Humpty Dumpty Was Pushed

And Other Cracked Tales

Bruce Lord
Elisabeth Richards

To Arden & Claire

Merry Christmas

Much Joy Always!

Bruce
Lord

Dec 2010

iUniverse, Inc.
New York   Bloomington

Humpty Dumpty Was Pushed

And Other Cracked Tales

iUniverse Star
an iUniverse, Inc. imprint

iUniverse books may be ordered through booksellers or by contacting:

iUniverse
1663 Liberty Drive
Bloomington, IN 47403
www.iuniverse.com
1-800-Authors (1-800-288-4677)

Because of the dynamic nature of the Internet, any Web addresses or links contained in this book may have changed since publication and may no longer be valid. The views expressed in this work are solely those of the author and do not necessarily reflect the views of the publisher, and the publisher hereby disclaims any responsibility for them.

ISBN: 978-0-595-47691-6 (pbk)
ISBN: 978-0-595-71559-6(cloth)
ISBN: 978-0-595-91955-0 (ebk)

Printed in the United States of America

Humpty Dumpty Was Pushed And Other Cracked Tales

Bruce Lord
Elisabeth Richards

To our parents, our first storytellers ...

Imagination is more important than knowledge.

Albert Einstein

The facts don't count because they don't make you laugh.

Leslie Weiler, age six

Contents

Humpty Dumpty Was Pushed

"He was a good egg. He was one of those salt-of-the-earth kind of eggs. He was a hard-working egg, a loving egg, a generous, kind and thoughtful egg, and he will be greatly missed." Chicken Little, like everyone else, agreed with those sentimental words spoken at Humpty's funeral. Humpty had been a good egg, and Chicken Little's best friend. What Chicken Little could not agree with, however, was what he was hearing everyone say after the funeral regarding how Humpty had died.

Chicken Little's outrage had started three days earlier, long before Humpty's funeral, when he'd read a very simple notice in the paper stating

> Humpty Dumpty sat on a wall.
> Humpty Dumpty had a great fall.
> All the King's horses and all the King's men
> Couldn't put Humpty back together again.

Most people read the notice and thought that it did little to capture the greatness of Humpty's life, the uniqueness of his character, the way his gentle presence brought smiles to all around him. In short, they felt the announcement failed to capture how Humpty Dumpty's all-too-brief existence had made the world a better place.

For Chicken Little, it wasn't just that the notice failed to express the greatness of Humpty that made him so angry. He was angry because the notice was a bold-faced lie. Chicken Little could barely contain his anger, but he knew that he would have one chance to inform the public of the truth … after Humpty's funeral when everyone was gathered at the wake.

Chicken Little spent the three days between reading Humpty's obituary in the paper and attending his funeral gathering evidence by talking to some key witnesses, double-checking his facts, and taking some high-resolution photos of where the alleged accident had taken place. He wasn't going to have a reoccurrence of the last time he attempted to sway public opinion.

The sun finally rose the morning of the solemn day, and everyone who was anyone came to pay their respects for their lost friend. There was Little Jack Horner, the entire Bo Peep family, Little Miss Muffet, Georgie Porgie, Jack Spratt and Peter Peter Pumpkin Eater, to name a few. Even Old Mother Hubbard, who was rarely seen in public these days, came to say goodbye. Each one of them knew exactly how Humpty had radiated love and joy into the world. They knew their lives had been enriched by knowing him. For miles around, crowds of people made the long journey to pay their respects. So many people came, and not just people.

Mary's little lamb tagged along bleating sadly. Turkey Lurkey and her sad little gobbles could be heard amidst the crowd. The cow took a break from jumping over the moon to moo her last respects. Countless other mourners came, too many to name here. They cried together. They listened to solemn words together. They consoled each other. They said goodbye as best they could in a funeral service that would be remembered by all who attended that day for its beauty and sorrow. Of course, Chicken Little was there as well, seething in his seat, waiting for his chance to speak.

After the funeral, as was the custom in their village, everyone gathered to reflect and celebrate Humpty's life. They gathered to tell stories and, oddly enough, to eat, as though funerals somehow made everybody hungry. They devoured by the handful little roast beef sandwiches, cheese and tomato sandwiches, tiny cucumber sandwiches, even peanut butter and jelly sandwiches. Perhaps not that surprisingly though, given the circumstances, the small mountain of egg salad sandwiches were left uneaten. Only Old Mother Hubbard hid a few under her hat for later, and if you had seen the state of her bare cupboards, you'd most likely have forgiven her. Of course, between bites of sandwiches and the many stories told of Humpty's childhood, of his famous wall-sitting adventures and of the funny things he had said or done, it was inevitable that talk would turn to his fatal accident, and when it did, Chicken Little was ready.

"It was a pity he had that great fall," said Jack Be Nimble. "But you know Humpty; he just couldn't stay away from a good wall. It was always one wall higher with him. First it was the Berlin Wall, and then remember when he sat on the Great Wall of China?"

"Yup, Humpty certainly was a risk taker," said Georgie Porgie after kissing Bo Peep and making her cry. "I can't help but think that at least if he had to leave us, he left us doing exactly what he loved most. Ya know, just sitting on the edge of some high wall that none of us would dare sit on, just soaking it all in."

"You're right there, Georgie," said Jack Be Nimble. "He loved heights and he loved a good challenge. You remember that mountain climbing expedition he took with those four other eggs they never found again? Humpty was the first and only egg to ever conquer Mount Fuji and live to tell about it."

Chicken Little seized his opportunity and marched up to Georgie Porgie and Jack Be Nimble. "I heard what ya said, Nimble, and I'm telling ya, you got it all wrong."

"Go away, Little," said Jack Be Nimble.

"Humpty didn't fall." Chicken Little was not going to be sent away. "I know everyone wants to believe that, but it's just not true. Humpty was pushed." Chicken Little's voice was a little too loud not to be overheard by several mourners nearby, one of them being Humpty's mother.

Mrs. Dumpty spoke up through her tearful sobs. "He was the bravest egg in the basket." With each word her voice came closer to cracking. "A real role model for the children. Always encouraging everyone to go for the top, to sit on higher and higher walls, and ultimately to conquer the wall within. Who would want to push my son, my beautiful boy? Everybody loved Humpty! How dare you make a mockery of his tragic accident! How dare you say such stupid, hurtful things!" Mrs. Dumpty slipped into uncontrollable, angry sobbing and was rolled outside where she could get some air.

For a moment, silence wafted through the room as people just stared at Chicken Little, feeling the awkwardness of the moment as they watched a sobbing Mrs. Dumpty leave the building. Jack Be Nimble used the silence to chastise Chicken Little so everyone could hear, "Nicely done, Little. See what you've done now! Why don't you just go home?"

But Chicken Little was far from ready to go home. He spoke in a voice that was meant for many more people than just Jack Be Nimble, and a crowd did seem to gravitate toward Little as he continued to speak. "It's not possible," Chicken Little began. "It's just not possible. It wasn't raining. It wasn't snowing. There's no way Humpty just slipped and fell. Think about it. You all know he wasn't just some amateur wall sitter. He was the best, the greatest wall sitter of all time."

Jack Horner shouted out in agreement. "Ya, Little's right; it couldn't have been just an accident."

Little Bo Peep put her arm gently around her friend. "I know it's hard to imagine, Jack, but try not to think about the accident. Think of happy days instead, when

Humpty would dress up as a giant Easter egg and take us on those Easter egg hunts. You remember?"

Little Jack Horner shook his head. "No, Bo, I don't want to be cheered up. I just want to understand what happened."

"He just fell. It happens," she said. Little Bo Peep was speaking more to Chicken Little than to her friend.

"I just can't accept that," Chicken Little replied. "Humpty had been up that wall hundreds of times. He knew that wall like the back of his hand."

Little Bo Peep asked him directly, "What are you saying, Little? Spit it out. This ought to be good."

"I'm telling you, beyond a shadow of a doubt, Humpty Dumpty was pushed!" he said.

"Pushed?" said Bo Peep. "Who would push Humpty? I don't believe it."

"You better believe it," replied Little Jack Horner. "Chicken Little's right. It's the only answer that makes any sense."

At that same moment, Georgie Porgie joined in the conversation. "Come on, Jack. Chicken Little has never made a lick of sense in his entire life."

"This is different," said Jack Horner.

"And you're gonna believe that nutbar? The same chicken who last year squawked for a month that the sky was falling?" asked Georgie. Then, looking around the room and lowering his voice, he added, "Besides, rumour has it that Humpty had some serious gambling debts. If you ask me, he jumped."

Little Miss Muffet was standing right next to Georgie Porgie. "Jumped!" she shouted. "He didn't jump. Humpty had everything to live for. He was getting his Hallowe'en costume ready, and I know he was excited about his chance to win best costume again."

Georgie rolled his eyes. "You mean that silly giant egg costume?"

"Yes."

"But he *was* a giant egg," protested Georgie.

"I know," said Little Miss Muffet. "That's why it was so convincing. He was just so happy, you should have seen the smile on his face . . . priceless. I know he was looking forward to the next costume party. No way he jumped."

"Then what, you think he just slipped and fell, or do you think he was pushed too?" asked Georgie.

"I don't know anymore. I guess maybe we should give Chicken Little a chance to explain why he thinks Humpty was pushed," said Little Miss Muffet.

Chicken Little wanted to explain right then and there, but other people were joining in the debate and it was getting a little out of control. Old Mother Hubbard and Jack Spratt were standing to the right of where Chicken Little was and near enough to Little Miss Muffet to add their thoughts regarding her suggestion.

"You heard the guy earlier," started Mother Hubbard. "It was an accident and all the King's horses and all the King's men will verify that."

"I never thought you'd be so naive, Mother Hubbard. You really think the King's men aren't capable of hiding the truth?" asked Chicken Little.

Jack Spratt seemed to agree with Chicken Little, "Ya, I think the King's men pushed him and then didn't even try to put Humpty back together again. What I'm thinkin' is the King's men caused the accident and then, under the King's orders, sent scrambled Humpty to the King's chef to make the biggest and tastiest omelette in the land. That's what I'm thinkin'."

Chicken Little tried to regain control of the conversation. "Will you just listen to me for a second?"

"They probably ate him for breakfast," continued Jack Spratt, ignoring Chicken Little.

"That's insane," said Little Miss Muffet.

"Hey, life can be pretty insane from time to time," added Georgie Porgie.

Mother Hubbard would not be swayed. "No. It's madness, plain and simple. He lost his balance and fell. End of story," she declared. She was feeling slightly guilty about the few egg salad sandwiches still under her hat and wondered, if only for a second, if they weren't possibly made from leftover giant omelette.

"He was pushed, and I have proof. Will you just stop and listen to me?" asked Chicken Little. But no one did. Since he could not stop them from talking, he left the disagreeable gathering more than a little frustrated and looked for someone who might listen to his evidence.

Across the room from Mother Hubbard's ongoing disagreement with Jack Spratt, Georgie Porgie and Little

Miss Muffet, Chicken Little saw his opportunity. Jack (of Jack and the Beanstalk fame) was recounting to Peter Peter Pumpkin Eater (of pumpkin-eating fame) Humpty's many wall sitting adventures during his long and glorious career as a professional wall sitter. "I remember as a little kid Humpty saying to me, 'You know, one day, Jack, I'm gonna do it. I'm gonna sit on the Great Wall of China.' I told him when I grew up, I'd climb a giant beanstalk and wave to him."

"I remember seeing pictures of Humpty sitting on the Great Wall of China in the paper. It was a big deal back then. Hey, did you ever get to wave to him from your beanstalk?" asked Peter Peter Pumpkin Eater.

"No," said Jack with a bit of a tear in his eye. "The thing is, he actually was sitting on the Great Wall just about the time I found that dumb old beanstalk. I tried waving to him, but it was just too cloudy that day so he couldn't see me. Later, he showed me all the pictures of himself sitting on the edge of the Great Wall, smiling that big goofy smile of his." Jack sighed. "I can't believe he's gone."

"Me neither. He certainly was one of kind when it came to wall sitting," said Peter.

"He was the best," said Jack. "I remember when he outsat the Japanese wall sitting champion, Nozumo the Flat-Bottomed, for the world title."

"That was a great day," said Peter.

"That was an amazing day," said Jack. "What people seem to forget is it took Humpty three weeks to outsit

Nozumo the Flat-Bottomed. Humpty sure taught him a lesson."

Chicken Little caught the last half of their conversation as he approached them. "Hey, Little! What's this nonsense I hear you're the one going around spreading rumours that Humpty Dumpty was pushed?" asked Peter Peter Pumpkin Eater.

Chicken Little had years of experience with not being believed and thus his feathers were not ruffled by Peter's question. "It's not nonsense, but I really doubt that a foolish pumpkin eater would understand."

"Oh ya?" said Peter. "Try me."

"Fine," Chicken Little began. He was relieved. Finally, someone was willing to really listen to him and he could share the awful truth of Humpty's demise. "You know that Humpty was a spokesperson for the Egg Board, right?

"Ya, I always thought that was a little bit weird, but what's your point?" asked Peter.

"Weird or not, Humpty was helping me research a story I was writing for the paper, and he discovered that all those expensive omega-3 eggs that are being sold by the Egg Board actually don't have one drop of omega-3 in them. Not one single drop. It's all a scam worth millions, and he was going to give me all of his evidence the day after his accident."

Peter Peter Pumpkin Eater shook his head. "You want me to believe that the Egg Board had Humpty eggsassinated?"

"That's exactly what I want you to believe," answered Chicken Little, "because that's exactly what happened."

"You really are too much, Little," said Peter.

"By the way, where's your wife?" asked Chicken Little. "I didn't see her at the funeral."

"None of your business!" snapped Peter Peter Pumpkin Eater. "Leave her out of this."

Just behind Peter Peter Pumpkin Eater, Mary and her little lamb were eating the last of the cucumber sandwiches. Little Boy Blue was asking her what she thought about what Chicken Little had just said. With her mouth still full, all she could mumble was, "I don't know. I don't care. I don't want to talk about it." This only made Little Boy Blue sadder and he left to find somewhere to fall asleep and make his sadness disappear.

Peter Peter Pumpkin Eater raised his voice at Chicken Little. "And what about all the King's men trying to put Humpty back together again? Huh?"

"They didn't really try, did they!" said Chicken Little. "Just another smokescreen, more media propaganda. Actually, they were more interested in crowd control than saving Humpty. From what Jack and Jill told me, and I interviewed them at length, the King's men just stood around and did nothing to save him. I don't even think they were the King's horses and King's men. I think they were Egg Board Investigators dressed up to look like the King's horses and King's men."

"Really! Now you're saying the EBI were in on it? Who's next? The CIA? The KGB? The RCMP? Well? Why not throw in the YMCA while you're at it? Sheer lunacy, Little. Whatever you're on, you really should up the dosage," said Peter.

"All I know is what Jack and Jill told me. They'll swear in front of a grand jury that they saw a bunch of EBI guys up on the grassy knoll near the wall just before the 'accident,' and there were more EBI guys nearby, back and to the left of the wall, and they were also up to no good," insisted Chicken Little.

"That's the most ridiculous thing I've heard in, well, since you were running around last year shouting to everyone, 'Oh no, the sky is falling.'"

"My timing might be off, but trust me, pal, whatever you want to call it these days, 'global warming,' a 'climate crisis,' whatever, the sky is still falling, and we better do something about it or millions are doomed. But that can wait until tomorrow; today, I need you to understand what happened to Humpty."

"Give it up, Little. There's no grand conspiracy behind Humpty's tragic accident," said Peter Peter Pumpkin Eater.

"You'll see. I'll show you. I'll show all of you," squawked Chicken Little. "Just you wait until the story breaks in next week's paper. Just you wait until the headlines read *Humpty Dumpty was Pushed*." Chicken Little left the wake in a huff, disappointed because no one was willing to listen to him yet again. His outburst was quickly attributed to his being distraught, and very few gave it a second thought.

Eventually, as the sun started to set, people left for their own homes to resume their lives. The last thing they saw as they left that day was a golden memorial egg timer that had run out of time. Beside the egg timer was a picture of Humpty Dumpty sitting magnificently on his favourite wall. On his face, a beaming smile that radiated joy into the world. This was a joy that filled everyone's heart as they left, a joy that would long outlast Humpty and become his legacy.

As people fell back into their daily morning routines, brushing their teeth, desperately hunting for their missing sock, wolfing down a quick breakfast of bacon and scrambled eggs, life went on as usual. Everyone, though, felt a little diminished and at the strangest times would notice the absence of their beloved Humpty. A few people, remembering the commotion Chicken Little had caused a week before after the funeral, and more out of curiosity than anything else, looked for the published proof Chicken Little had assured them would be printed in their morning paper. They looked for a hard-boiled expose on page one denouncing the omega-3 scandal but could find none. They looked throughout the rest of their paper for a detailed account of the Egg Board's involvement in Humpty's death and the clever conspiracy to cover it up, a theory only a madman like Chicken Little could hatch in the first place, but not a word about that could be found anywhere. Unfortunately, no one would ever see that proof published, if it existed at all. What they did find, however, was a rather surprising tiny story detailing Chicken Little's untimely death.

Apparently, from sources undisclosed, Chicken Little had been driving at top speed, hurrying to the newspaper to publish some article, when he drove through a freak hailstorm. With hail the size of eggs falling from the sky, he crashed into the very same wall that Humpty had fallen from just a week before. This was at least the *official* version of Chicken Little's death. Unfortunately, his passengers in the back seat, Jack and Jill, did not survive the crash either. The details were rather sketchy, but certainly Chicken Little's reporting days were now officially over. Those who recall Chicken Little's outrageous claims still sometimes speculate if there was any truth behind his allegations, but their questions will forever remain unanswered.

Cazador de Estrellas de Mar

(The Starfish Hunter)

There once was a man who lived by the sea. His skin was dark and briny, his eyes the color of salt water and his lips like two pieces of cracked leather. The people in Cuba called him Cazador de Estrellas de Mar because he hunted stars on the beach.

For years, people would stand around him in amazement as he talked about his recent starfish adventures. Some were so impressed that they would offer him a portion of their day's catch.

"How clever you are, Cazador de Estrellas de Mar," they would exclaim as they showered him with lobsters and crabs.

The years wore on, however, and all too soon Cazador de Estrellas de Mar was an old man. The crowds grew tired of his starfish stories and visitors to his shack became fewer and fewer until the stream of people became a

15

trickle. The trickle turned into a few drips, and the drips themselves seemed one day to almost completely dry up.

After a long drought of loneliness, a small boy stumbled upon Cazador's sea shack. Astonished by all the starfish that coated the sides of Cazador's shack, the boy decided to pay the old man a visit.

"Go away," said an old, grumpy man from inside the shack.

The boy flinched slightly as he smelled the strong scent of sugar coming from within. Determined to speak to the old man, he said cheerfully, "I'm told you are Cazador de Estrellas de Mar, the great starfish hunter."

The door of the starfish shack swung open and the old man glared into the boy's eyes. "I do not know that man of whom you speak." The man took a swig of some pink Kool-Aid from the bottle he was holding in his hand. "My name is Cazador," he growled, "that is all, nothing more."

"But, Cazador," exclaimed the boy, "you are a legend in our land. I have heard my grandfather speak of you many times."

"A legend?" The deep lines in the old man's face faded slightly, as if the sails in his wrinkled skin had been filled with a soft wind. Looking at the boy more closely, he cleared his throat and added gruffly, "You can come in if you want."

The boy entered the small, rundown shack, noting all the various specimens of starfish that sat around the room. "Wow, a starfish hat, starfish boots. You even have a starfish belt!"

The boy looked at the one and only picture on the wall, faded now after so many years. It was a dancer, a Flamenco dancer, one of the most famous that ever lived but long before the boy's time. "Who is that?" the boy asked. "She's beautiful."

"That, my curious boy, is none other than Siobhan the Magnificent, the greatest Flamenco dancer that ever lived, as lovely as she was talented."

"Was?" The boy looked closer and saw in her hands two castanets made out of starfish. "What happened to her?"

"No one knows for sure but most say she ran away with pirates; some say she became a pirate herself." Cazador looked at the picture and seemed to speak to it as much as he was speaking to the boy, "Wouldn't really surprise me if she was captain of her own pirate ship by now, just look at those eyes, so dangerous and so diabolical." For a moment, Cazador looked younger himself as he stared into the painted woman's eyes until the boy interrupted with another question.

"Did you give her those starfish?" he asked.

"Yes," said Cazador, "before her final performance, before she was lost to the world forever. I only saw her use them once."

The boy heard a hint of sadness and loss in Cazador's voice, so he asked a question to turn the conversation to an entirely different topic. "Cazador, why do you kill starfish?"

The question certainly brought Cazador back from his nostalgic revelry. "Why do I kill starfish? Because they're deadly, that's why," said Cazador as he crawled up onto his hammock. "Oh sure, starfish may seem harmless enough in an aquarium, pretending to be slower than a snail, but I know better. Those things can leap six feet in a single bound and bite you before you can say scallywag."

"Bite you?" the boy asked.

"Yes, bite you," sneered the old man. "Starfish are the cobras of the sea, a deceptive and clever species, amassing their army so they can take over the world." The old man thought for a moment and then added, "At least up to the shoreline."

The sitting boy hugged his knees. Unsure of what to make of the old man's story, he decided to question him further. "I can see how a starfish might bite you, but attack you?" The boy shook his head. "It just doesn't seem possible."

"Oh, it's possible alright," said the old man, gritting his teeth. Motioning the boy to come closer, he growled, "If you're not careful, a whole posse of them will sneak up behind you and eat you alive." Then the old man pulled up his pant leg and showed the boy two tiny star-shaped red scars on his big toe. "Do you see these? One of those starfish nearly finished me off. Though the chomp of a great white shark might be quite painful, there's nothing more agonizing than being slowly eaten alive by a starfish."

The boy inspected the bite, his eyes growing wider with interest. "Cazador, have you ever actually seen anyone killed by a starfish?"

The old man answered, "No, but I've heard about it from a friend of a friend who knew this guy who saw a starfish kill someone named Howard."

"Oh," said the boy meekly as he dumped a small lizard out of his shoe. After a long silence, the boy pointed toward a large harpoon standing against the wall. "I guess you kill them with that?" he asked.

"Yes," said Cazador as he sat back in his hammock looking at his harpoon with great affection. "I remember the great battle I had with that vicious group of starfish from Havana. I was about ten feet from the shoreline when I knew I was in trouble. Just me and six starfish, and only one harpoon left. Sure I could get one of them, but then it would be five of them on me, unarmed. I was only safe if each one of them thought they could be next." Cazador took a deep breath in, as though the starfish were still standing in front of him. "So there they were, their legs stiff and dangerous looking, each one of them poised to jump on me, but I managed to make them hold their distance. I backed onto the sandy beach as they backed into the ocean, but I knew I would meet them again one day."

"And did you kill them?" the boy asked.

"Yep, eventually," said Cazador with a wide grin.

The boy gazed out at the sea through the window and saw the great surf pounding the shoreline. Turning his head back toward the old man behind him, he asked, "Has there ever been a starfish that you didn't catch?"

"Yes." The old man sighed, his grin beginning to fade. "There was one starfish that I never caught. They call it the Great Pink."

"Is it big?"

"Big? It's huge, massive, almost the size of a baby seal." The old man looked up at the ceiling and took another swig of his Kool-Aid. "One night I woke up and the Great Pink was stuck to my cabin window. I could hear him laughing at me through the glass, mocking me. And then, with one of his tentacles, he waved at me before he jumped back into the water. I tell you, I didn't get a wink of sleep that night."

The boy squinted at the old man who was now sitting in complete darkness. "How come you never caught it?"

The old man stared at his gnarled hands. Squeezing them tightly, he said sternly, "I think you should go now." His voice was like broken glass.

Reluctantly, the boy got up and walked toward the door, "Adios, Cazador de Estrellas de Mar. It was nice meeting you."

As the boy left, a man met him just outside the shack. "Tiago, what are you doing? We've been looking all over for you!" he said.

"I was just talking to the Great Cazador de Estrellas de Mar," Tiago protested.

The man folded his arms across his chest. "Cazador de Estrellas de Mar is nothing but an old sugar-drink drunk who likes to tell tall fish tales. I wouldn't waste another breath talking to that foolish old man." He grabbed Tiago by the shoulder and marched him away from Cazador's shack.

"An old sugar-drink drunk who tells tall fish tales!" shouted an outraged Cazador from inside his shack. Far away, he could hear the Great Pink laughing at him once more. Picking up his harpoon, he smashed the half-empty Kool-Aid bottle on the ground and declared, "I must have his bumpy hide!"

For the next 85 days, Cazador trained and planned to capture the Great Pink. Every day, he would ride on the backs of his two trusty dolphins, Flipper and Guppy, to scout out various sections of the ocean. He mapped out the north and the west quadrants of the nearby sea. He began to strengthen his mushy muscles by weightlifting two giant shrimp. "I can feel that starfish getting closer, scuttling across the silent ocean floor," Cazador would mutter to himself as he continued lifting the shrimp over his ears. It was on the 86th day of his intense training, while lifting shrimp on the beach, that Cazador finally saw the tip of the Great Pink's head just a few feet from the shoreline.

"That's him!" Cazador cried out as he dropped his shrimp and quickly slipped on his starfish spurs.

Now normally a starfish hunter attracts starfish using a particular dance. It starts off by putting a left foot in and taking a left foot out and then putting a left foot in and wiggling it all about. This dance continues for several hours until the wiggles have completely left one's body. Once the hunter is wiggle-free, the person's arms and legs will naturally go all stiff and stick out like a star. Then, the person must make the sound of a lonely, lost starfish, a sound somewhere between the noise of a dying giraffe and the haunting growls of a seasick otter.

But to match wits with the Great Pink, Cazador de Estrellas de Mar, the Great Starfish hunter, could not rely on these ordinary methods. Instead of being visible on the shoreline, he quickly covered his body with sand. And rather than making the noise of one lonely starfish, he made the noise of three lonely starfish.

There was a steady breeze from the west that day as the starfish hunter waited for his prey to come ashore. He watched the Great Pink's head slowly emerge as he wriggled his way onto the beach. Waiting until the last possible second, Cazador leapt up from beneath his sandy camouflage, reached for the harpoon at his side and prepared to strike.

Fate, however, was not with the old man that day, as the wind suddenly picked up and blew sand into his face. "Curses," he howled as he wiped his eyes. "I cannot let that starfish escape again!" So the starfish hunter, semi-blinded by sand grit, followed the Great Pink, who, being startled by Cazador, had begun running as fast as he could down the length of Varadero Beach. "The Great Pink is cruel and intelligent," said the old man as the tears fell from his face, "but I am crueler than he."

Soon the old man's tears were mixed with rain, as a tropical storm began to whip the trees to and fro. Several large bugs bit him in the behind, but he marched on.

He lost his shorts in the wind, but he marched on. A dirty diaper blew into his face, but still he marched on.

This went on for several hours until finally Cazador began to grow tired. With his muscles at the point of breaking, the old man fell to his knees, defeated, and bellowed, "That's it, starfish. You win. I cannot fight you any longer."

Surprisingly enough, when Cazador de Estrellas de Mar spoke those words, the starfish stopped running. The Great Pink turned and slowly approached the kneeling old man. Then, with deliberate slowness, the Great Pink reached out with one of its legs and saluted the old man as any arch enemy would do for a worthy adversary. The old man smiled slightly, and the starfish did a small respectful farewell dance. And then, the Great Pink submerged itself once more into the depths of the sea.

The old man stood alone on the seashore that afternoon. There was no one to watch his great battle with the pink sea monster, no one to witness their moment of truce, but somehow he didn't care. Cazador lay down to sleep that night under a palm tree, and for the first time in years, he dreamt of nothing but the clear blue sea without a single starfish in sight.

Billy and His Tragic Nose Hair

While there are no medical textbooks written on the subject, there are some diseases that are known only to teachers, and Billy had one of the rarest: *speedius nosehairius*. As cases of bad nose hair go, Billy had the worst. It grew at the alarming rate of 17 inches a day.

At first Billy tried trimming it, but he just couldn't keep up. He sought medical treatment, but that didn't work either. Nose specialist after nose specialist had no choice but to throw their hands in the air, shrug their shoulders and walk away. One doctor did try to be a little more helpful than the others, but it wasn't quite the cure Billy was hoping for. He gave Billy the rather unorthodox advice that he'd be best off if he ran away and joined a traveling circus.

While Billy was not quite ready to join the circus, it would be fair to say that it was hard for him to return to school, as he did not like being different from all the other children. He was, in fact, so ashamed of his wild nose hair that during class he would try to stuff it back up his nose so that others wouldn't see it. Sometimes he would attempt to shape his nose hair into a long handlebar moustache even though it fooled no one. When people passed Billy in the hall, they would make fun of his nose hair, and they never let poor Billy join in any non-nose hair related games.

"I hate my nose hair," Billy said to his mother one day.

"Oh, Billy, you mustn't think of your nose hair that way," she said. "It's part of you. You must think of it as a special gift."

Billy thought long and hard about what his mother had said. It took a very long time indeed. In the end, though, Billy thought that perhaps she might be right. Perhaps he could put aside all of his anger and embarrassment and accept his unique gift. Perhaps it was special. Perhaps he was special. Perhaps, one day, his nose hair would make the world a better place.

So Billy began to display his nose hair proudly. He also began to use it to make things. At first, he made only small things, but soon Billy became quite the craftsman with his nose hair. For his father's birthday, Billy made an entire chess set out of densely woven nose hair. For his mother's birthday, Billy knitted a nice pair of nose hair winter mittens and a matching nose hair scarf. His parents were so pleased with their gifts, they were speechless.

Becoming increasingly bold, it wasn't long before Billy found his true niche: the Guinness Book of World

Records society. There he met all kinds of people with special gifts, and like Billy, they were also very generous. Someone gave him a pair of homemade 16-inch fingernail earrings. Someone else gave him pieces of fish scales right off her elbows that Billy could use to decorate his nose hair crafts. A kind elderly woman lent Billy an extra pound of earwax so he could shine his shoes. Billy became close friends with all of them.

Billy's life was going just great until that very sad day when he rode the escalator. Billy had let his nose hair grow 152 feet long and was mere inches away from winning the World Nose Hair Championship. Feeling rather pleased with his overabundant nose hair locks, he let them dangle on the floor. This was extremely unfortunate, as some of Billy's nose hair got caught in the teeth of the escalator. Billy found himself being pulled into the moving steps and about to be turned into a great big mound of furry hamburger. He thought to himself how sad it was that he would die without ever being victorious and that his nose hair nemesis, Sven Smorgensteen, would be crowned the World Nose Hair Champion. But Billy did not die that day, and Sven would not be crowned king.

Though Billy's nose locks were the reason for him being pulled into the escalator, they were also the reason why Billy escaped with only minor injuries. As Billy felt himself being dragged into the machine by one of his lengthy nose locks, he quickly made his other nose lock into a loop and lassoed the emergency off lever and was saved.

While recovering in the hospital, a very concerned Dr. Sprain said to Billy, "Young man, you are lucky to be alive." Billy kissed the one nose lock that saved his life. Dr. Sprain continued firmly. "But as you can see, your nose hair is a safety hazard."

Billy jerked his head forward. "But, doctor," said Billy, "there is nothing I can do about *speedius nosehairius*. It just grows too quickly."

"That's where you're wrong, young man," said Dr. Sprain with a grin. "There is a Romanian doctor I know who can cure you. Your nose hair will never grow again."

"Never grow again?" Billy looked stunned. Being normal? This was beyond his wildest dreams. Or was it? He looked out the window and imagined a future without nose hair.

"Well?" asked Dr. Sprain.

"I can't do it," said Billy. "I need my nose hair! I love my nose hair!"

"Suit yourself," said Dr. Sprain. "But I'd advise you, next time, take the stairs."

Many years passed, and Billy became a household name. He had become the World Nose Hair Champion soon after he had left the hospital. Billy used his fame as a springboard to successfully market his own nose hair clothing line. It took many years, but Billy went on to beat all kinds of nose hair records. He held the personal nose hair knitting record for knitting three million pairs of nose hair socks and four million pairs of nose hair underwear, all surprisingly more comfortable than one might at first imagine. Billy had even developed a line of deluxe nose hair sleeping bags and had plans to develop some nose hair pajamas.

After all his success, when Billy was an old man, a doctor came to visit him. It was the same doctor who had treated him for his escalator injuries over fifty years before. Even though the doctor's face was now wrinkled like a raisin, Billy recognized the wizened old man instantly. "Dr. Sprain," said Billy excitedly as he wrapped his nose hair around his body like a shawl. "It's been so many years. Please, come in and sit down."

"Why thank you, Billy," said Dr. Sprain as he entered the house. The doctor crossed the room and slowly sank into the cushions on Billy's nose wool couch. "Billy, I have a confession to make."

"What is it, Dr. Sprain?"

"Many years ago, when you were my patient, I stole a hunk of your nose hair while you were sleeping."

"No problem," Billy replied with a chuckle. "I always have plenty of nose hair to spare."

"But the good news is," Dr. Sprain continued, "I have performed many experiments with your nose hair. Combining it with the wings of some fruit flies from Thailand, old pieces of pizza from my fridge, and some nitroglycerin, I have used your nose hair to create a fertilizer that people can use on their heads. We call it *Ever-grow*."

Billy looked confused. "I don't understand."

"Billy, we now can use your nose hair for hair transplants. Bald people, movie stars with bad toupees—

think of all the people that will benefit from your nose hair fertilizer."

"Wow," said Billy. "My nose hair really will help to make the world a better place."

Billy and Dr. Sprain chatted for a few hours and then it was time for Billy to say goodbye to the good doctor. As Billy watched the doctor walk down the road, two stray kittens playfully pawed at his dangling nose hair. When the doctor was no longer in sight, Billy came inside, looked at a picture of his mother and said, "Thank you, Mom; you were right." Billy then went off to bed and tucked his valuable nose hair in for a good night's rest.

Fredrick the Seasick Sailor

Ever since Fredrick was a child, he had always wanted to be a sailor. His father was a sailor. His grandfather had been a sailor. Even his great-grandfather had been a sailor. Naturally, Fredrick wanted to be a sailor too. Fredrick yearned to follow in their footsteps, but there was one small problem. He got seasick. A lot.

"Well," Fredrick thought to himself, "if I'm ever going to become a sailor, I'm going to have to get over this."

After pondering his problem for quite some time, Fredrick decided the best place to begin was his house. In his bathroom, he hung a shower curtain with seashells on it and placed a small raft in his bathtub. In his living room, he put a large rowboat on the floor and ate dinner in it while listening to sounds of seagulls and ocean waves on his iPod. His friends, when they visited, rocked pictures up and down so that Fredrick would feel as though he were on board a ship.

After years of these exercises, Fredrick felt he was ready to face a real ocean. He went to sailing school, earned his sailor's degree, and soon after, headed out to sea.

Unfortunately, Fredrick's first sea assignment was not aboard an aircraft carrier or a battleship. It was not aboard a cruiser or a destroyer. His first assignment was the HMS *Impossible*, a tiny and barely seaworthy craft. The HMS *Impossible* was so light that when waves rocked the boat, people's stomachs would toss and churn like milkshakes in a blender.

"People have died aboard this ship," said one of the crew, sucking up the saliva from his parched lips.

"Why did they die?" asked Fredrick.

"Because they got so seasick," slurped the crewman. "They threw themselves overboard just to end the madness."

Fredrick looked wistfully at a tree disappearing on the horizon.

"So this is our new swabby?" boomed a cannon-like voice.

"Aye, aye, Captain," said Fredrick to a great hulking man with two rotten teeth. It was the one and only Captain Jack Pigeon. On his arm was a large tattoo that read, "Death to Seasickness." Fredrick nervously asked, "What would you like me to do first? Grab the steering wheel? Look at the radar screen? Polish the anchor?"

Captain Jack scowled. "What rank are you, youngin'?"

"Able-bodied seaman, first class," said Fredrick proudly.

Captain Jack was unimpressed. "Yes, well able-bodied seaman, first class, you're first duty is to help our cook prepare a mouth-watering dinner for us."

"Cook?" It hadn't occurred to Fredrick that there were other non–sea related duties that one might have to perform on a ship.

"Yes, cook," snarled Captain Jack. "Now go down to the mess hall and help whip up a pot of fish gut soup. For a side dish, I'll have some whale-eye Jell-O and some dumplings in a squid ink gravy. For dessert, bring me some of those dainty little shark brain tarts I like so much. And if we're out of tarts, then just make some eel heart pudding, heavy on the eel."

Fredrick's face turned green. "Surely, you must be joking."

Captain Jack was not smiling, "Young man, in the 27 years as captain of this vessel, I can assure you I have yet to crack a joke, and don't call me Shirley." Then, the captain paused for a moment and grabbed Fredrick's chin in his hand. "You're looking a little green there, sailor. You wouldn't happen to be seasick, now would you?"

"No, sir," said Fredrick.

"That's good," said Captain Jack, as he let Fredrick go. "Now get de-braining."

So Fredrick went down to the bowels of the ship and, for three hours, diced 100 shark brains and minced 100 whale eyes. After putting everything onto some silver platters, he went to bed sick and exhausted.

The next morning, Fredrick went up to the deck to see what new duties he would be assigned. "Well," said Captain Jack as he scratched his chin, "your first duty today is to pick the lice out of the men's beards."

Fredrick's mouth dropped open in disbelief. "But, Captain!" he exclaimed. "Lice are disgusting. Can't somebody else, perhaps another able-bodied seaman with more experience, do it?"

The captain's eyes grew large and red. "What! You think you're above all that, able-bodied seaman? You think you're too good for some de-lousing? Well, on my ship you'll do what you're told, understand?" Captain Jack slammed his fist on the table to reinforce his point.

"Yes, Captain," replied Fredrick meekly.

"And one more thing," said the Captain. "Yesterday, I lost the tweezers when I used them to clean out my belly button lint. So you'll just have to de-louse the men's beards with your bare fingers."

So Fredrick and the ship's doctor got all the men to sit down in a line, and one by one, they began to de-louse their beards. And the more Fredrick de-loused, the sicker he got.

"Say, sailor," said the doctor, as he grabbed a louse and squished the little tyke between his thumb and forefinger, "you look a little green around the gills. Are you sure you're not seasick?"

Trying not to look at the growing pile of lice bodies at his feet, Fredrick murmured, "Positive."

"That's good," said the doctor. "The last seasick sailor jumped overboard and was eaten by sharks." Fredrick looked overboard to see just how many sharks might be waiting for him to jump.

"I will not be seasick. I will not be seasick," said a determined Fredrick under his breath.

"Ah, I see that you've finished de-lousing the men's beards. Excellent!" said a voice from behind. It was Captain Jack. "Now it's time for you to clean out the garbage cans," he said.

"Garbage cans?" asked Fredrick.

"Yes, garbage cans. Now I'm not going to lie. It's not going to be a fun job . . . certainly, not as much fun as de-lousing. Many of those garbage cans haven't been cleaned for over a year. And if I know my garbage cans, they're probably crawling with fly larvae."

Fredrick's stomach began to turn upside down, "But, Captain—"

"No buts. Now get moving. Those fly larvae aren't getting any younger."

"I will not be seasick," said Fredrick as he opened up the garbage cans. Now, if Fredrick had to describe the smell, he might say that it was a mixture of rotten eggs, decaying fish intestine, moldy cheese, decomposing fruit and something that smelled worse than Death itself. Of course, this would only begin to describe the stench that wafted into Fredrick's nostrils that afternoon. Bravely, he cleaned each of the garbage cans, one after the other, trying to ignore the larvae crawling up his arms, particularly the more athletic ones that were determined to reach the top of his head, like tiny mountaineers climbing their own human Mount Everest.

About five hours later, sick, exhausted and stinky, Fredrick crawled into his bed. Even the shower he just had could not entirely remove the smell of garbage. He had begun to think that the whole sailor thing was not such a great idea after all. It was with that thought Fredrick began to plot his escape.

The next day, Fredrick and the crew enjoyed a day of shore leave on a small island. For lunch, they ate some turtle waffles, with a choice of chocolate or raspberry sauce, and later enjoyed a nice cup of cocoa. At five o'clock, everyone returned to the ship—everyone, that is, except Fredrick.

"Sailor!" shouted Captain Jack, slamming his cup of cocoa down on the railing, "Why are you not onboard ship?"

Hiding up in a coconut tree, Fredrick yelled back to the captain, "Because I'm landsick."

The captain scratched his head. Never before had he heard of someone getting landsick. "What nonsense! Get on board this ship now," he demanded.

"Okay, Captain, whatever you say, but it might kill everyone," Fredrick said.

"What are you talking about? Is it that serious?" Captain Jack asked with noticeable hints of worry in his voice.

"Yes," said Fredrick, "your eyes explode and then in three days you shrivel up into a pile of goo."

"Sounds messy."

"Very messy, and it's highly contagious!" Fredrick warned.

"Oh!" uttered the captain. "In that case, I guess we'll have to leave you on this island."

"Perhaps that would be best," Fredrick agreed.

"Sorry about your luck, sailor. You had great potential and you'll be deeply missed." Captain Jack turned his back on Fredrick forever and headed out to sea.

"Goodbye," said Fredrick, greatly relieved. As the ship's smoke disappeared on the horizon, Fredrick began to wander around his newly found paradise. He whistled a happy tune and then went for a bath in a nearby pond. "Finally clean," he said. "And no seasickness." Fredrick wiped the cool water off his body, got dressed and lay down on a bed of palm leaves. He fell fast asleep.

When Fredrick awoke, he heard the sound of two giggling women. "Sailor, oh, sailor," they cried.

Fredrick rubbed his eyes. There, right in front of him, were two beautiful mermaids.

"Sailor, do you know who this island belongs to?" asked the first mermaid.

Fredrick shrugged his shoulders. "I don't know. To everybody I guess."

"Silly sailor, this island belongs to us," said the second mermaid.

"Oh," said Fredrick. Noticing just how lovely the two mermaids were, he asked sweetly, "Do you think you would mind if I also lived here?" Fredrick smiled his most charming smile and added, "I *am* very fond of fish."

The two mermaids whispered to one another for a few seconds. "Yes," said the first mermaid, "you may live here, but only on one condition."

"What?" said Fredrick, grinning from ear to ear. "I'm sure that I can meet your one teeny-weeny condition."

"Well," said the first mermaid as she winked at the second, "you'll have to pull the barnacles off our tails, cook our favourite meals, including slug soup, scrub down the pond scum and basically do anything and everything we ask."

"Yes," agreed the second mermaid, "for the rest of your life."

"Yes," repeated the first mermaid, "anything and everything, always and evermore."

Fredrick looked out at the sea. Then he looked down at the pond scum. Then he looked out at the sea again. Then back to the pond scum. Then he looked at each of the beautiful mermaids. Then he looked at the pond scum once again.

"Well," Fredrick said. "at least you're both prettier than Captain Jack." So Fredrick the seasick sailor put down his anchor and gladly accepted his new job as official mermaid cleaner and groundskeeper. He spent the rest of his life cleaning and serving those two beautiful mermaids who were very pleased with Fredrick's work, very pleased indeed.

The Ear

Jenny was normal in every way, except one. She loved squeezing ears. Big ones, small ones, thin ones, fat ones: she didn't care.

As a newborn, she squeezed the ears of the other babies in the hospital. When she got home, she squeezed her mother's ears. Sometimes, when no one was around, she would even squeeze her own ears.

As she grew older, her desire to squeeze ears only grew with her. During breakfast, she often squeezed her younger brother's small elflike ears. At school, she would fondle the long fluffy ears of her classroom's pet rabbit. She would squeeze the ears of her classmates. Occasionally, she would squeeze her teacher's ears. Once, she even squeezed the principal's ears. When she came home after school, she spent most of dinner staring at her father's ears. When dinner was over, Jenny would try to enjoy at least one squeeze of his elephant ears. Even when she slept, Jenny would dream of squeezing ears, thousands and thousands of delicious ears.

Of course, everyone asked Jenny why she had to keep on squeezing their ears. Most often Jenny would reply, "Just because," but once in awhile she'd reply, "It's fun, you should try it." Jenny simply loved squeezing ears, but telling people this did not make it any easier for them to understand or accept her ways.

"Dad," Jenny's brother would cry, "she's looking at my ears again!"

"Jenny!" yelled her father. "Stop looking at your brother's ears."

"But, Dad," Jenny protested, "they look so tempting. I just want to reach out and squeeze them a little."

"Obviously, we are going to have to do something about this ear squeezing of yours," said Jenny's father sternly. And they did do something.

Jenny's brother grew his hair over his ears down past his shoulders, effectively hiding them from her squeezing fingers. Her father began wearing earmuffs inside the house all the time. The school rabbit did not have to hide its ears because Jenny had squeezed them so much that one day, unfortunately, they fell off. Even still, Jenny continued her ear-squeezing way of life.

By the time Jenny was eight, she was cutting pictures of ears out of magazines and pasting them all over her bedroom walls. By the time she was nine, she was studying medical textbooks on the ear. By the time she was ten, Jenny had read all of Vincent van Gogh's letters to his brother Theo and had, using plastercine, made a perfect copy of Vincent van Gogh's dismembered ear. She named the plastercine ear "Little Vinnie" and slept with it under her pillow. Sometimes she would take it to school in her coat pocket, and squeeze and talk to it when no one was looking.

Gradually, others were converted to her ear-squeezing ways. After school, Jenny started the Secret Ear-Squeezing Society. When the students met, they would sit on large ear-shaped beanbag chairs and have ear-squeezing contests. Whoever could tolerate the most ear-squeezing without screaming or crying won. They even created their own secret magazine called *The Ear*.

Eventually, Jenny left home and went to university where she naturally studied to be an ear massage therapist. And for the rest of her days, Jenny happily lived out her dream, squeezing her patients' ears, living in her ear-shaped house, swimming in her ear-shaped pool, sleeping in her ear-shaped bed and drinking coffee from her ear-shaped mug.

Sir Stinks-A-Lot

In a kingdom by the sea lived a valiant knight who truly lived up to his name, Sir Stinks-A-Lot. He was both loved and despised by everyone in the kingdom. Loved, as Sir Stinks-A-Lot had saved them from many dragon attacks and bands of spear-waving barbarians; despised, for the methods that he used to protect their lives.

Legend has it that Sir Stinks-A-Lot had slain 39 dragons without ever lifting his sword. In the famous battle at Castle Flung Gungpoo, with the wind at his back, Sir Stinks-A-Lot single-handedly stopped 3000 invading barbarians by simply raising his arms. Even King Arthur's Knights of the Round Table, brave as they were, were not brave enough to stand downwind of Sir Stinks-A-Lot and his fearsome stench.

No one really knew the origins of his stinky power. Some say Sir Stinks-A-Lot was born behind a pigpen and that his father was half skunk, half man. Some insist that he spent the first six years of his life crawling and walking about wearing the same dirty diaper. Others contend that Sir Stinks-A-Lot simply refused to bathe and would never put a washcloth to his face. Whatever the truth, it was shrouded in a stinky cloud of mystery.

While many praised Sir Stinks-A-Lot as a hero in the kingdom, he truly was the loneliest hero in the land. No one would invite him to dinner parties for obvious reasons. The one time Sir Stinks-A-Lot was invited to a dinner party, years ago, the dinner guests passed out during the first course, overcome by stink exhaustion. Sir Stinks-A-Lot ran out of the castle humiliated once again. Even after he had left, the entire castle reeked of rotten eggs and dirty socks for weeks. Word spread throughout the kingdom, and that had been the last formal dinner party Sir Stinks-A-Lot ever attended.

So Sir Stinks-A-Lot, lonely as he was, resigned himself to slaying dragons with his stench and protecting the kingdom on his own from afar. Thoughts of love and settling down with some beautiful princess had long left him. He was happy enough in his dragon slaying. And luckily, his only friend, Sir Smelgar, who for some strange reason was immune to the powerful attack of Sir Stinks-A-Lot's infamous odour, kept him company from time to time.

One day, Sir Stinks-A-Lot set out on a routine dragon assessment tour, roaming from mud shack to mud shack, searching for signs of recent dragon activity in the area. While galloping on his trusty steed, a noble horse whose nostrils where covered by lemon-scented burlap strips, Sir Stinks-A-Lot caught a scent wafting through the air. It was a scent more beautiful than rotting fish, more thrilling than sour milk, more mysterious than old garbage.

"What is that enchanting smell?" excitedly asked Sir Stinks-A-Lot.

Sir Smelgar, riding beside his smelly companion, flared his nostrils and inhaled deeply, "Yes, I see what you mean. Rather overpowering, isn't it?"

At that moment, a woman walked by carrying a basket of vegetables, a container of milk, a loaf of bread and a stick of butter. Noticing two men raising their noses in her direction, the woman, known in her kingdom as Stinkerella, hung her head in shame. Like Sir Stinks-A-Lot, she too lived up to her name and had also lived a lonely life of smelly despair and embarrassment. Wanting to avoid any unnecessary bad-smell jokes, Stinkerella started running toward her castle. She headed for the safety of the quiet, dark dungeon where she could stink in peace and perhaps mend her lobster net after serving lunch to her cruel, noseless step-brother.

"After her," yelled Sir Stinks-A-Lot. "I must know more about the woman behind that smell. I think I'm in love."

And so Sir Smelgar caught up to the fleeing young woman and said, "Dear lady, my liege Sir Stinks-A-Lot wishes to meet with you."

Stinkerella merely lowered her eyes and said, "But my cruel step-brother is expecting me to make him his lunch."

"He will have to wait," replied Sir Smelgar. "Sir Stinks-A-Lot has smelt you, and he is not a man to be trifled with."

A look of fear mixed with hope crossed Stinkerella's dirty face. Could any man get past the wall of stink that surrounded her? She was curious and more than a little nervous. "Alright," she said, "I will meet this brave knight of whom you speak." Turning her head, she saw none other than Sir Stinks-A-Lot bended on one knee.

"Dear lady," said Sir Stinks-A-Lot, "your smell has captured my heart, and therefore, I request your hand in marriage."

"But, kind sir," sputtered the smelly maiden, "I'm an outcast in my kingdom. You would be marrying someone who would have to live apart from others."

Sir Stinks-A-Lot held Stinkerella's hand and said, "I would be proud to have you live in my castle. In fact, I will buy you another castle that is far away from the world of sniffing noses. There you will be safe from the hurtful words that people hurl at you like slings and arrows."

And so the two stinky people were married in a stinky ceremony, and they rode off in a giant rotting pumpkin carriage. Soon after, they moved into their new castle that was, even according to medieval standards, a bit drafty.

Eager to spruce up their new homestead, Sir Stinks-A-Lot took out a copy of *Ye old Home Hardware Manual* and began to seal up some of the holes in the wall.

In the midst of these repairs, a seven-inch dragon appeared out of a hole in the wall. "Hey, get away from my lair," cried the puny creature.

Sir Stinks-A-Lot was startled. "Who are you?"

"I am Zandar, the mightiest soap dragon in the land, and I demand that you leave at once, or I will have to remove you by force."

Sir Stinks-A-Lot nearly keeled over with laughter. "You, a puny seven-inch dragon, do battle with me? What are you going to do, roast my big toe?"

The tiny beast snarled. A small soap bubble escaped its left nostril.

"Alright then, prepare to be attacked," said Sir Stinks-A-Lot as he lifted his arms in anticipation of an easy victory. Expecting the dragon to faint within seconds, Sir Stinks-A-Lot was astonished when nothing happened. "Why are you still standing?" he asked.

"Because I am a soap dragon," Zandar replied, "and you are a rather stupid, stinky knight." The dragon sized up his enemy and found him lacking. "Now you will feel my soapy wrath. Prepare to be cleansed." Zandar breathed forth many frothy bubbles.

"Ouch!" Sir Stinks-A-Lot shouted. "Quit it! That hurts!" The bubbles felt like acid as they burst upon his stinky ankles. Tiny clean spots soon appeared on his flesh as the relentless bubble attack continued without mercy.

The bubbles multiplied and rose higher into the air. Sir Stinks-A-Lot was helpless. He tried to scream, but his mouth was full of soap bubbles. Sir Stinks-A-Lot reached out for a more conventional weapon, a sword or an axe, but his eyes were blinded by the dragon's fearsome onslaught. In a gargled voice, Sir Stinks-A-Lot at last cried, "I surrender. You may live in your dragon hole in peace." The dragon seemed satisfied with the terms of Sir Stinks-A-Lot's surrender and left him alone.

The next morning, Sir Stinks-A-Lot awoke only to find a strange odour coming from his skin. "Sir Smelgar," he called to his friend in the next room, "come here and smell my armpit. It seems to be a bit off."

Sir Smelgar burst through the door in knightly fashion and obediently put his nose up to Sir Stinks-A-Lot's armpit. Inhaling deeply, he said, "Hmmm, yes. I see what you mean."

"What is it?" inquired Sir Stinks-A-Lot. "Swampy milk? Rotten tangerines?"

"No, I think," Sir Smelgar took another whiff, "it seems a little more like lilacs."

"*Lilacs!*" Sir Stinks-A-Lot was beside himself. How could he be the most powerful dragon slayer in the land if he went galloping around smelling like lilacs?

Moments later, Stinkerella came through the door, "Ah, did my husband have a good night's sleep?" Stinkerella's eyes began to water as she waved her hand in front of her nose. "What is that dreadful smell?" she asked.

Sir Stinks-A-Lot cringed. "I had a fight with a soap dragon. It did not go so well."

"Ohh," she said as she began to swoon, "I think I'm going to faint."

Sir Stinks-A-Lot caught his wife just as she was about to fall to the ground and he lay her gently on a bearskin rug. "Sir Smelgar, I cannot have my beautiful wife being upset with me. Therefore, I must ask you to help me get back my stinkiness."

And so with Sir Smelgar's assistance, Sir Stinks-A-Lot tried a variety of ways to regain his special odour. He swam with skunks. He put on garlic as deodorant and padded his armour with onions and mouldy cheese. He spent a week lying on a 50-foot garbage heap and used sewer rats as pillows. He wore the same pair of socks for a month. All his attempts, however, were unsuccessful.

"Will I never stink again?" he cried to the heavens. Looking back at the castle, his heart was heavy with sadness. He knew his wife would never be happy if she was married to a sweet-smelling prince.

With the scent of lilacs still upon his skin, Sir Stinks-A-Lot walked slowly back to his castle to grab a few things and say goodbye. He found his wife crying, alone, in the castle dungeon.

"Goodbye, my wife," he said as he kissed her hand. "I cannot ask you to suffer for one second more."

His grieving wife placed her hand upon his cheek. "My darling, I don't care if you smell like disgusting flowers. I love you. And nothing, no fragrance, no matter how soft or sweet, will ever come between us." Then she put her arms around his neck and said, "Kiss me, my fragrant fool." And in that kiss, something magical happened. Sir Stinks-A-Lot's stench returned to him tenfold, and the two of them began their life afresh in a stinky heart-shaped cloud of togetherness.

The tiny seven-inch soap dragon looked on from his tiny dragon hole, and he could not help but be moved to tiny tears of soapy joy.

The Girl in the Hat

Once there was a small, rather ordinary girl who lived in Japan. She said ordinary things and walked in an ordinary way. But there was one thing about her that was not ordinary: her large straw hat.

Now to the average person, her hat was just another hat. It was large. It was made of straw. Sometimes it was difficult for people to get around when they were trying to get on a bus or a train or into a canoe. But it was a hat nonetheless.

To a small frog named Musashi, however, it was far more than just a hat. It was the home of his dreams. He knew he must live in that hat no matter what the cost. He planned and waited until at last an opportunity presented itself to him like so many deliciously cooked flies served on a silver platter. Not long after, on one blustery afternoon when a strong gust of wind blew the hat off the girl's head, he jumped into the hat and started hopping away.

"Hey!" yelled the girl as she chased after her hat. "Come back here!"

The frog seemingly did not hear her cry.

"Did you hear what I said?" asked the girl, finally catching up to the bouncing hat.

The frog lifted the hat up slightly so he could have a good peek at the hat's owner. "Oh, I'm sorry," said the frog, "Is this hat yours?"

"Yes, it's my hat, and I'd like it if you gave it back now," snapped the girl.

Musashi croaked, "But I don't have any place to live." Then he added in his best polite frog voice, "Would you mind terribly if I lived in your hat?"

The girl was taken aback. "But this is *my* hat."

"Oh, I see," said the frog as he put a flipper to his lips. "Then perhaps we could share?"

"Share?"

"Yes," answered the frog. "I don't weigh very much, and I'd be pretty good at keeping away the horseflies and mosquitoes."

The girl picked up the frog to see if he were indeed as light as he said he was. "Well," said the girl thoughtfully, "I suppose I could let you live in my hat as long as you don't croak too much and keep me up at night."

"I'll be no trouble at all," said Musashi. "You'll see."

So the girl allowed the frog to live on the brim of her hat. Though seeing a living frog on top of the girl's head raised the occasional eyebrow, most people just ignored the girl as they always had.

A few days later, a small bird named Himiko came down and landed on the girl's hat. The girl tried to shake the bird off her hat, but it wouldn't budge. "Please get off my hat," pleaded the girl.

Himiko tweeted, "But this nest gives me such a wonderful view." Then she swung upside down on the hat's brim and stared the girl straight in the eye. "How much do you want for it?"

"My hat's not for sale," the girl said firmly.

"Okay, okay," chirped Himiko. "How 'bout I give you six bugs . . . no, seven bugs . . . and a juicy caterpillar. It's a good deal. Oh come on, let me live here. I'd take up no space at all."

The girl sighed. "Alright, you can live on my hat as long as you don't make too much noise."

"And as long as you don't peck me," added the frog. So the bird, along with the frog, lived on the hat. This caused a couple more people to notice the girl, but everyone else still just walked on by.

A week passed, and a number of other animals asked to live on the girls' hat. This included a shrimp named Sae, a beetle named Hiroki, a lobster named Fat Larry, a small crocodile named Karate Lips, a land eel named Ryo, and a baby horse named T-Rex. So the girl in the hat walked down the street with a bunch of animals on her hat, and for the first time, large numbers of people began to notice her.

"Look at that girl!" exclaimed a passer-by.

"She must be famous!" shouted another.

And so more and more people on the street began to follow her and ask for her autograph. Pretty soon, photographers were snapping pictures. The girl with the hat's photo was shown on dozens of magazines including the cover of *Big Hats*. "World's Most Famous Person," it said. And wherever the girl went, she was swarmed with reporters.

"When did you first buy the hat?" asked one reporter.

"If you had to do it again, how would you wear it differently?" asked another. But the girl found all the attention very noisy and tiresome, so she began to flee from their questions.

"Look, she's running from us," declared a woman with large, black spy binoculars.

"That means she's extra famous," cried her colleague. "After her!"

The reporters and photographers chased the girl all the way home. The girl tried to escape, but everywhere she went she kept finding a reporter hiding in a garbage can or a photographer appearing from under the sink.

"This has to stop," said her father.

The girl looked lovingly at her hat. It was a fine hat, a very fine hat. Perhaps the finest hat she had ever worn. But it was just too popular. So, with great sadness in her heart, she took the hat and set it free on the back porch. When she did so, a big fight broke out in the girl's backyard and people began to bid on the hat.

"I'll give you one million dollars for that hat," said a tall thin man.

"Two million," yelled a slightly thinner man.

But everyone was too late, for as they were all busy fighting over the hat, a large rhinoceros came around and ate it. The animals living in the hat were lucky to escape with their lives.

"Oh no, the rhino has eaten the hat," lamented a reporter.

"Quick, let's take a picture and interview him," said another.

And so everybody left with the rhinoceros, and the ordinary girl was ordinary once more. Sitting alone at the kitchen table, the girl stared at her reflection in a spoon. Certainly, her parents seemed happy, but she was not. Something was missing. And then she realized what it was. "I miss my hat," said the girl sadly.

Her mother gave her a warm smile, put her arm around her and said gently, "Honey, that hat was nothing but trouble from the beginning. You knew you'd have to put it down sooner or later."

The girl said nothing and continued to stare at her reflection.

"One day you'll realize that this was for the best," sighed her father as he got up from the table.

Little did her father know that his own advice would be put to the test, for it was at that very moment that all the animals that had been living on top of the hat burst into the house.

"Here," squawked Himiko, "look what we made you!"

The girl's eyes widened only to discover that the hat inhabitants had made her a new hat, a brand new hat made out of newspapers, natto and pineapples.

"Oh, how extraordinary!" she gasped.

"And we promise not to live in it," said Fat Larry.

The girl raised her eyebrows. "But where will all of you live?" The baby horse looked at the lobster, the lobster looked at the crocodile, the crocodile looked at the frog and the frog looked at the girl's father.

"We thought that maybe we could live here," croaked Musashi.

"Here?" cried her father. "But this is my house!"

"Father," said the girl. "There's no point in arguing with them."

So the family agreed to let everybody live with them under their roof, and they all took turns wearing the extraordinary hat.

If a Whale and a Tiger

Margaret was a curious young girl. Everyday, she would pester her parents with questions like "What makes me, me?" or "Why is there a sun?" or "Why is water wet?" or even "How come green is green?" There was one question, however, that she asked more than any other: "If a whale and a tiger had a fight, who would win?"

Her father hated that particular question so much that he would hide under the breakfast table. When her mother heard it, she would start humming. She did this so often, Margaret became convinced that her mother was part hummingbird. Margaret's relatives and neighbours felt that they had the perfect solution. They pretended they were Swedish and could not understand her question. This did not stop Margaret, though, from asking it anyway. She was sure that somewhere out there, there was an answer.

Now some children are terrified of their first day of kindergarten, but not Margaret. She had heard so many wonderful things about school being a place filled with answers. She eagerly skipped to school to meet her unsuspecting kindergarten teacher, Mr. Smart.

Now Mr. Smart knew many things. He knew the answer to two plus two plus two. He knew how to draw circles without lifting his pencil from the paper. He even knew how to button up his red cardigan sweater with one hand. But Mr. Smart did not know the answer to Margaret's question, and that made him feel very unsmart.

Pushing his glasses back up his nose, Mr. Smart said, "Well, I'm sure your question is very important, little . . . what is your name again?"

"Margaret."

"Yes, Margaret, a very important question, but right now, we must all learn to tie up our shoes properly, so your question will just have to wait, okay?"

Margaret was disappointed, but she also knew that the school year was very long and that she'd have other chances to ask her question. That moment, unfortunately, never came. Just as Margaret would put up her hand, Mr. Smart would always have the students answer some other less-interesting question, like "What is the capital of China?" or "What time is it when the big hand is on the three and the little hand is on the twelve?"

Soon the school year was over, summer came and went, and Margaret found herself in grade one.

Mrs. Smiley was all smiles that first day when she met her grade one class. All smiles, that is, until she met

Margaret and heard Margaret ask, "If a whale and a tiger had a fight, who would win?"

Two fighting caterpillars replaced Mrs. Smiley's smiling eyebrows. "Young lady, that question is not really a real question, now is it?"

"But why?" Margaret asked.

"Because a whale lives in the ocean, and a tiger lives on land, so by the laws of nature those two animals can never meet."

At first, Margaret was paralyzed by the sheer logic of her teacher's response, but Margaret persisted. "But what if the fight was on the shoreline? What if the whale was still in the water and the tiger was at the edge of the water?"

"Or," another bright-eyed student offered, "what if they fought in outer space, and the whale had water inside its spacesuit instead of air?"

Other students began shouting out their ideas until Mrs. Smiley screeched, "Alright students! Question time is over!" The children fell silent. "Now," Mrs. Smiley continued calmly, "I suppose these things might be possible in some crazy land of make believe, but we live in the real world, and now it's time for us to return to our spelling." Everyone quietly took out their paper and pencils and Mrs. Smiley brought out her trusty marking pen in eager anticipation of some serious marking. Margaret had no choice but to return to her spelling as well.

Margaret went through each school year with satisfactory grades. She began to accept the routine bells and whistles that told her when to sit, when to eat.

and when to have fun at recess. And after awhile, she stopped asking her question. She got older. She went to college. She got a job. She wore a grey suit, walked down a grey sidewalk and worked in a grey building. Her parents were so proud.

One Thursday afternoon, Margaret stepped outside to eat her lunch. Sitting on a grey bench beside the grey sidewalk, Margaret looked up to see a bus drive by on the busy street. Something about the ad painted on the side of the bus caught her eye. It was a great big whale swimming toward a sign that read, "Come to Korea." The picture stirred something in her memory, but it began to melt like soggy cereal when Margaret realized it was almost time to get back to work.

As fate would have it, as fate sometimes will, a large hurricane in the Gulf of Mexico earlier that week had created huge air currents. The air currents forced a large number of barn swallows off course, pushed thousands of monarch butterflies into North American cites, and had caused one of those butterflies to land at that very second on Margaret's knee.

Margaret thought the orange butterfly was beautiful. The orange shimmering wings and the black stripes at the tips reminded her of something, but what?

"A tiger!" Margaret shouted. Then she thought of the ad on the bus, "And a whale!" Suddenly, Margaret knew what she must do. Dropping her half-eaten sandwich on the ground, she stood up and announced to the world, "I'm going to Korea. There, I will find an answer to my question."

So Margaret flew to Korea, and she met many interesting people who told her many interesting things. One evening, she heard about a monk from an old woman serving her some kimchi at a tiny restaurant in Seoul. She had asked Margaret why she had come to Korea, and Margaret had told her about her quest to find an answer to her question.

"Ah yes," said the old woman, "the whale and tiger question. Such an old question, and such a good one." She smiled and added, "You will need to seek the forbidden temple, located near Mount Ahn. Do not worry. It is less forbidden than it sounds. The temple is not far from the dreaded avalanche of truth, and rather near the forest of stinky land sharks. There, you will find your answer."

Margaret was afraid of making the journey, partly because what the old woman had said did not seem to make a lot of sense, but mostly because she was afraid that her question would never be answered and that her trip, if not indeed her entire life, would have been for nothing. So Margaret pushed on and followed the directions she had been given as best she could until seven evenings later, not long after sunset, she walked into the forbidden temple where she met a very old and withered man wearing a tattered orange robe.

"Margaret, I've been expecting you," said the old man.

Margaret was stunned that the old man knew who she was. "How do you know my name?" she asked.

"I know many things," said the old man, "and we have many things to discuss, but first you must shower, because, to be quite honest, you smell like a stinky land shark."

Margaret bathed, dressed, ate a pear and then she and the old man talked by torchlight under the stars.

"Your question is very interesting," said the old man. "Generation after generation of children have come here to ask it, but so far, you are the only adult that has been able to find their way into this temple."

Margaret's eyes shone bright as stars. "Can you answer my question?"

"Yes, I can," the old man replied confidently, "but why don't you tell me what you think the answer is first?"

Margaret could see something warm and gentle sparkling in his eyes. After thinking for a moment, she leaned forward and whispered in his ear what she thought the answer might be.

The old Buddhist monk smiled a marvellous smile and said, "You see? The answer was within you all the time."

And Margaret thought about how she had gotten on a plane to Korea, how she had climbed Mount Ahn, how she had avoided being trapped under the avalanche of truth, how she had escaped the stinky land sharks and how she had found and entered the not-so-forbidden temple. "Yes, I understand," said Margaret. And she did.

"Good," said the old Buddhist monk. "Now, go and live your life."

Margaret hugged the old man, thanked him and then continued on her journey. As she left the not-so-forbidden temple, it vanished into the Asian moon, waiting to reappear only for those daring enough to ask their question.

The Mosquito Farm

George Grunt lived in a small town called Slumberville. He was a poor boy who didn't have any friends. Needless to say, George was very, very lonely.

One night, a mosquito flew into George's room. George, being the lonely boy that he was, said to the mosquito, "Why don't you come in and stay for awhile?"

Of course, the mosquito, being the mosquito that it was, came over and bit George. But it was neither a very big bite nor was it too painful. George, therefore, was in no hurry to shoo the mosquito away. And instead of leaving through the window on its own accord, the mosquito decided to lie down quietly on George's forehead and fall into a restful sleep. All night, the mosquito dreamt of chubby little children with chubby little arms waiting to be bitten. What George dreamt of that night is still a mystery.

Next morning when George awoke, he found the mosquito sleeping soundly on his forehead. George said to himself, or perhaps to the mosquito, "A friend. My one and only friend." Then, noticing what might have been a yawn coming from the newly awakened mosquito, George pulled up his sleeve and offered his newest and bestest friend some breakfast. The mosquito was much obliged, and thus a new friendship was born.

The next night, a few more mosquitoes came through George's window. And just as he had done before, George offered them food and a place to rest.

Soon George's room was full of mosquitoes. In fact, it was so thick with mosquitoes that the air above George's bed looked like a tiny black cloud. But this never really bothered George because the mosquitoes never drew that much blood and were, for the most part, remarkably quiet and polite.

His father, however, did not share George's enthusiasm for his new swarm of friends. "Those pock marks on your arms can only mean one thing," said his father as he spread a giant blob of jam on a piece of toast, "a mosquito farm."

George fell silent.

"Yep," continued his father, "I've seen you up there trying to get them to come in with your night light."

George looked at his father's mouth, which was now full of toast. Realizing that his mosquito farm could no longer be kept secret, George clasped the edge of the kitchen chair tightly between his fingers and asked, "Can I keep them, Pa?"

"Nope."

"Please, Pa, they're my friends."

"For now," said his father as he grabbed a can of Buzz-Off from the cupboard. "But mark my words, boy. One day, those mosquitoes are going to turn on you." Then his father handed him the Buzz-Off and said, "Kill them son, while you still can."

George backed away from the can.

"If you don't kill them, I will," said his father.

George took the can half-heartedly and went up to his bedroom. He knew his father was right. Of course, knowing what one has to do and doing what one has to do are often two entirely different things. When George went into his bedroom and saw that all of his friends were happily buzzing around his bed, he couldn't bring himself to squeeze the trigger.

"Maybe I can just scoot all the mosquitoes outside and close the window instead," thought George. But George thought wrong. Many of the mosquitoes did not want to leave and became quite upset when he tried to capture them in glass bottles.

"Ouch," said George as one mosquito gave him a vicious bite on his neck. He then danced around the room like a grasshopper as 50 others flew up his pant legs.

"Alright, I'll let you stay!" yelled George. Instantly, the attacking mosquitoes retreated out of George's pants. "But you have to promise not to turn mean again."

The bugs seemed content with his words and went back to happily buzzing above George's bed. George felt that he had reached an agreement with the mosquitoes and that everything would be just fine.

The next morning, a strange old man was sitting at the breakfast table.

"Who are you?" asked George.

"I'm your father," said the old man angrily. "Those darn mosquitoes of yours bit me so badly they drained my body and turned me into an old man."

"No way," said George.

"I told you to get rid of those mosquitoes, and what did you do? You kept them alive, didn't you? Let them grow stronger, didn't you?"

George hung his head in shame. "I'm sorry, Pa. I should have listened to you."

"Shhhh, quiet!" George's father cupped his hand to his ear and whispered, "Can you hear that?" George's eyes darted in the direction of a whining sound coming from the front door. "Those mosquitoes are up to no good, I can sense it."

"What are we going to do, Pa?'

"Only one thing we can do, son. We're going to have to call in the Skeeter Busters."

"Who are they, Pa?"

Twenty-seven minutes and a number of odd seconds later, George's question was answered. Three men wearing body armour burst through the Grunts' back door. The first was carrying a three-foot bazooka. The second was carrying 100 pounds of TNT. And the third was carrying a small pair of nail scissors.

"Skeeter Busters at your service," said the man with TNT. "What seems to be the trouble?"

George's father shamefully spoke from the table, "My boy here tried to raise a mosquito farm."

The man with the nail scissors nodded his head knowingly. He turned to the others, clenched the scissors tightly and said, "It's worse than we expected, boys, a full-fledged skeeter farm. Tell home base this is an official alpha-1 alert. I repeat, an alpha-1 alert."

George looked at the men's radioactive hunting suits, which were mosquito in color and covered with asbestos wings. "Are those clothes heavy?" he asked.

"Very," said the man with TNT. "Now you'd better stand back, as we still don't know what we're dealing with."

"Better do as he says," said George's father.

Although curious to know more about the silver-clad men, George obeyed his father's instructions. Once he and his father were standing safely in the corner of the room, the men began to unpack their equipment.

The Skeeter Busters were outfitted with an odd assortment of danger-related gadgets. One of them looked like a bouquet of underfed Venus fly traps. Another seemed like a pair of badminton racquets coated with extra-strength flypaper. A third gadget was an ultra high-tech robot frog with laser tracking eyes and a heat-seeking tongue.

"Alright, men," said the man with the bazooka, "let's do a full area sweep. Arnie, I need you to turn on your motion trackers."

"I'm on it, Bazooka Joe," said Arnie as he put down his pile of TNT.

"And Teeney," continued Bazooka Joe, "I need you to leave one drop of blood in front of the air vent. We're gonna do this old school."

"Aye aye, sir," said Teeney. He took out his nail scissors and gently pricked his pinkie.

"What do we do now?" asked George's father.

"Now we wait for those skeeters to get hungry," said Bazooka Joe. "Teeny's blood is some of the tastiest in the country." A single drop of blood fell on the floor right in front of the air vent.

"Yup," Arnie agreed, "skeeters mostly like to feed on Teeny, mostly."

The hungry mosquitoes responded as expected. Soon the low mosquito humming in the distance turned to a nearby dull roar. Noticing the red blips multiplying on his motion tracker, Arnie shouted, "Joe! I'm getting multiple signals."

"Where?"

Arnie glanced at the screen in front of him, "Looks like they're inside the room."

"But that's impossible," said George's father. "We'd see them if they were inside."

"Better go infrared, men," said Bazooka Joe. "And seal the doors if you have to." Teeney and Arnie took out a blowtorch and began to seal every door in the kitchen. After five minutes, it was clear that no one would be getting in or out of the room.

"I'm still getting motion," shouted Arnie.

"Where are they!" yelled Bazooka Joe.

All of a sudden, a horrible whining noise was heard from the sink. "The pipes!" The pipes!" hollered Teeny. "We forgot to seal up the pipes."

"Stay calm everyone," said Arnie.

"Duck and cover!" shouted Teeney.

As the mosquitoes poured out of the kitchen drain in droves, the three men quickly dove for cover under the table and consulted each other as to what their remaining options were. "I guess we could blow ourselves up," said Teeny. "At least that way, we'd take the skeeters with us."

"No, there's civilians present, and we haven't lost a civilian yet," said Bazooka Joe.

"Wait!" said George as he ducked his head under the table and joined the Skeeter Busters, "I've got an idea."

"Son, get back to your dad and keep low," said Arnie.

But George didn't listen. Instead, he ran in clear sight of the mosquito swarm to the cabinet and got out a piece of paper and a big black marker.

"George!" shouted his father, "don't be a hero!"

"Whatever that kid's doing, it better be quick," said Teeny as the black cloud began to thunder around his head.

George wrote furiously on the paper, taped it to the fridge and opened the freezer above. The three Skeeter Busters read the note and smiled at the young boy's cleverness. The mosquitoes read the sign as well, which said in big letters, "Mosquito Ice Rink—Free Skating Today."

Now, while most people know that mosquitoes enjoy attacking people in swampy places, what they might not know is that mosquitoes are avid skaters, quite literate, and most of all, the insect world's best bargain hunters. So, when the mosquitoes read the free skating sign that day, they naturally rejoiced, went into the freezer and began skating in a frenzy. Once George was sure that every last mosquito was in, he shut the freezer door and waited until each and every last mosquito was frozen solid.

"You did it!" cheered George's father as he threw his arms around his son. "You outsmarted those mosquitoes!"

"Did you see how they all went in there?" said George excitedly as he pointed toward the freezer.

"Nobody touch nothin'," said Bazooka Joe. Instructing Arnie and Teeney to decontaminate the kitchen and unseal the doors, he began to wrap the freezer in a black, tightly bound industrial cling film.

"What are you going to do with that freezer? Blow it up?" asked George's father.

Bazooka Joe almost smiled at the thought and simply replied, "That's classified and a matter of national security, so I would remind you as far as telling anyone about these skeeters, you just tell them they were never here."

"Never here?" asked George's father.

"That's right. Never here," said Bazooka Joe.

The men carried the freezer to their truck and finished gathering their equipment. Just as they were about to depart, the man with the bazooka turned to George and said, "Clever work youngster. If you ever need a job, you know where to find us. We're in the book." George smiled as he watched the three men climb into their armoured truck, drive off toward the sunset and seemingly disappear into thin air.

The Last Action Librarian

Out of all the dolls children bought, Suzy was the most popular. She had long blond hair and blue eyes, and she came with many accessories, including an airplane, a pool, a camper, a tennis court, a cell phone, a pony, a health membership and a thousand other items too adorable to mention.

And Suzy had the perfect mate, called Cam. Like Suzy, he was perfect looking. He had tanned skin, blue eyes and the body of an Olympic athlete. People said they looked perfect together. They spent a great deal of time together enjoying walking around and commenting on how perfect they both looked when they passed a reflecting surface. They did not talk about much else. This bothered neither of them and they continued living their perfect little lives until one day tragedy struck at the very heart of Suzy and Cam's togetherness.

At first when Suzy noticed that Cam was missing, she was not overly concerned. He was probably just running late. She looked in her airplane and in her camper, but Cam wasn't there. "I wonder where he could be," she thought to herself. "Maybe he's pinned down under some heavy weights at the gym." But she knew that Cam was too muscular to be pinned under any weights. Suzy waited and waited, and grew impatient. "He's supposed to help me wash my fabulous hair." She pouted to her reflection in her Sparkle-Deluxe Suzy beauty mirror.

A few hours passed, and when Suzy found a ransom note in her mailbox, her impatience turned into worry and dismay. It was a picture of Cam with his arm removed with some words scribbled underneath. "Oh, my poor handsome Cam," she thought. "How will you wash my hair with only one arm?" Suzy tried to decipher the writing under the picture of her one-armed Adonis. "If only I could read this note and figure out where you are," she thought to herself as she stumbled over the words. After a few more minutes of struggling, Suzy decided that she needed some help.

But finding someone to help her read the ransom note was going to be much more difficult than she had originally thought. Bambi and Binki, her best friends, could read little more than the instructions on their bottles of hair gel. "They're just too popular," sighed Suzy. "What I need is a brainy doll that stays home every Friday and Saturday night and reads." Suzy tried to remember the other less-popular dolls that sat beside her in the store and were never bought by anyone. "Let's see," she said as her finger twisted a long strand of blond hair, "there was Tina Tae-Kwon-Do, Egghead Ernesto and of course

Jimmy the Journalist." Suzy started to rub her temples. "Oh, this thinking is so difficult." Then, just as she was about to give up and go back to polishing her nails, Suzy was struck by perhaps the greatest idea of her life. She would go to school and learn how to read. It was certainly beyond most Suzy dolls' wildest dreams, but something told her it was the only choice that made sense.

The next day, Suzy got up at 5:00 AM, spent two hours putting on her makeup and then enrolled in the Beverly Hills Silicon elementary school. Although her designer classified her as 18, she was put into a grade one class with many monsters and assorted baby dolls. The teacher seemed very surprised to see Suzy there.

"In all my years of teaching," said the teacher doll, "I've never seen one of the Suzy lines in my class."

Suzy patted her nose with some powder and said, "Well, I guess there's a first time for everything, isn't there?"

"Yes, I suppose there is," said the teacher doll dryly. "Now, shall we begin with our lesson?"

"Oh, just a minute," said Suzy. "I have to call one of my friends." And Suzy began dialing her illuminated cinnamon-peach cell phone.

"Give me that!" snapped the teacher doll as she snatched the cell phone out of Suzy's hands.

"Hey!" squealed Suzy. "You can't do that. My cell phone is part of my identity. I mean, what's a Suzy doll if she doesn't have a fabulous cell phone and thousands of friends to call?"

The teacher gave Suzy an unsympathetic smile. "I guess you'll just have to buckle down like everybody else."

Suddenly, Suzy, who always had a permanent smile on her lips, looked upset. "Oh my goodness," she said aloud. "I wonder if I'm wrinkling up."

Taking out her mirror for the 20th time that morning, she inspected her face like a fashion model inspects her non-fat, low-cal, decaf, no foam chai tea latte. As she did so, the teacher said to her, "Suzy, why don't you stop preening in the mirror and try to read what's up on the blackboard."

Suzy seemed stunned. Usually, people let her do whatever she wanted and asked nothing from her in return. Squinting her eyes as she looked at the blackboard, she said, "Sssssss."

"'Sssssss' is not a word," said the teacher.

"But 's' is a very scrumptious sound, is it not?" said Suzy looking around the room to see if any boys were watching her.

"Oh yes it is!" said an undereducated Lizard Man action hero who threw himself at Suzy's feet.

The teacher doll was infuriated. "Suzy, it's obvious that you don't know how to read, so I'm sending you down to our librarian so you can get some special assistance."

Suzy smiled. She liked being thought of as special.

After an hour of going in and out of various bathrooms to check her makeup, Suzy finally made it to the library.

"Ewww," said Suzy, "what are all those drab things on the wall?"

"Those would be books, deary," said a woman who was reading a noticeably extra-thick book. Having heard that books were dangerous things that ruined your eyes and left you wrinkled, Suzy prided herself on never having seen a book, let alone having touched one. That is why it seemed quite odd to her that the woman should be reading a book with such interest.

"Um," said Suzy, not quite knowing what to say in a non-party environment.

"Is there something you need help with?" the librarian doll said as she reluctantly closed her book.

Suzy stared at the woman. She had chunky glasses and her hair was in a tight bun. Her stockings had fallen down around her puffy ankles and her shoes had no heels. "Wow, do you ever have bad fashion sense," said Suzy.

"I'm a librarian doll," said the woman. "Fashion does not interest me. Literacy, reading, knowledge, these things interest me. Now, have you come here to read something or have you come just to make superficial comments and waste my time?"

"Super . . . ficial. What does that mean?"

The librarian doll shook her head. "It's the kind of childish comment that an empty-headed Suzy doll makes." Then the librarian doll began reading where she last left off.

Suzy was stunned. Whenever people talked to her in the past, they usually were so pleased to meet her. Overwhelmed by her insights on the weather, overjoyed by her latest tossed salad recipe, overexcited by her off-the-rack fashion advice, people always were delighted to be in her presence. Never before in Suzy's life had she been ignored by someone else, and she felt sad, but not in that normal "Oh no, I've missed a 50 per cent–off sale on high heel shoes" kind of sad. This sad was strangely more disturbing.

After two minutes of silence, Suzy finally broke down. "Okay then, teach me how to read."

The librarian doll looked up from her book and declared, "Now we are getting somewhere." Pointing toward the bookshelves, she added, "Let us take the first step of our journey. We will begin where we must begin, at the beginning, with *Green Eggs and Ham*."

"I'm scared." Suzy shuddered.

"I would expect nothing less," smiled the librarian doll. "Fear is the great educator. The gateway to your future is shelved up there. "

Suzy tried to see the book that the librarian doll was pointing toward. "I can't see it," said Suzy.

"Of course you can't," said the librarian doll. "Only librarian dolls are designed to see up to seven decimal spaces from 20 feet." The librarian doll climbed the bookshelf and brought the book down.

"Holy cow," said Suzy. "How did you do that?"

"Super strong arms and extra stretchy legs for climbing bookshelves—another feature of a librarian doll."

Just then, two boys started chatting very loudly in the library.

"Shhhhhhhhhh," said the librarian doll with her powerful shhsh-er. The boys' chairs were blown back five feet from the table. One of the boys complained that he could no longer hear out of his left ear. Satisfied that the library was once again silent, the librarian doll opened before Suzy the magic of Dr. Seuss.

"Just a minute," Suzy interrupted. "I have something that I need you to read first." Suzy pulled the ransom note out of her pocket and handed it to the librarian doll. "Someone has kidnapped my darling Cam!"

"A kidnapping, eh?" The librarian doll inspected the note with a large magnifying glass. "Yes . . . no . . . yes . . . no . . . YES!"

"What is it?" asked Suzy anxiously.

Whipping her glasses off in classic superhero style, the librarian doll said triumphantly, "These letters are out of a book from this library!"

Suzy did not understand the connection. "So what does that mean?"

"It means that the kidnapper is someone who attends this school."

Suzy frowned. "But hundreds of dolls attend this school. How can you find out who it is?"

A small smirk escaped the librarian doll's lips. "Simply by locating the book and finding out who was the last one to take it out."

As the librarian doll walked over to the computer, another student entered the library. It was a Wendy doll, a grade four student who was designed not to do her homework.

"Well, well," said the librarian doll harshly to the newcomer, "if it isn't Wendy. I haven't seen you in this library for at least three months. Got lost looking for a candy store, did we?"

Wendy's face began to turn ketchup red. "I meant to come here earlier, honest."

"A likely story," snapped the librarian doll. "Why must you turn my library into a house of lies?"

Wendy wailed, "I'll read more in the future, I promise."

"Good. Now go over to that table, be silent and read," said the librarian doll strictly. "And whatever you do, don't dog-ear the pages. Books deserve respect."

"Yes, ma'am," said Wendy as she quickly got out a book and began reading.

The librarian doll sighed. "Now where was I?"

Filing her nails, Suzy looked up casually and said, "You were about to go to the computer to find out who wrote that ransom note."

"Oh yes," said the librarian doll. "And put that nail file down," she added crossly. "This is a place of learning, not a beauty parlour." Suzy pouted, and then put the file back into her purse.

The librarian doll quickly found the information she needed. "Here it is. That book was taken out by Carla Cunning."

"The Cunning series!" Suzy exclaimed. Suzy had fought with that line of dolls ever since she came out of the factory. There was the classic battle in the camper, and then the extra-long tennis match in which Suzy almost died of chapped lips. "I don't think Carla has any intention of returning Cam," whined Suzy. "She's always had eyes for him."

The librarian doll scratched her chin. "Looks like we'll need backup." Grabbing Suzy's cell phone, the librarian doll called Tina Tae-Kwon-Do.

"Will she help us?" said Suzy.

"Yes, Tina is always up for fighting injustice," said the librarian doll. "Now off to the book mobile."

Twenty minutes later, Suzy, the librarian and Tina arrived at Carla's house. Tina motioned to Suzy and the librarian doll to go to the front door. "You guys distract her while I go out back and look for Cam." Then Tina Tae-Kwon-Do did a karate chop through the bushes and disappeared.

"Hello," said the librarian doll as she knocked on the door, "anyone home?"

The doorknob turned slightly and then an eye peered from within. "What do you want?" said the voice. The voice apparently belonged to a young lady with bright pink lips.

Trying to push her way into the house, Suzy shouted, "Cam, I want Cam."

"There's no Cam here," said the voice and the door swung shut.

"It was her!" cried Suzy. "It's Carla. I'd know that lipstick colour anywhere!"

While Suzy and the librarian doll discussed what they should do next, Tina had slipped around the back of the house and was in the midst of rescuing Cam, who was tied to a fencepost.

Tina undid Cam's gag and freed his hand from Carla's trap. "I'm suffering from dry mouth and wrist burn," he said weakly. She picked his other arm off the ground and popped it back into place. "That Carla is one evil doll." Then Cam pointed to all the candy wrappers spread out around his feet. "Will you just look at all the fattening foods she was feeding me? It's amazing I didn't end up with a bad case of acne. I must have gained at least three pounds."

Tina was surprised by Cam's first words, particularly as none them seem to include a "thank you." As she continued to free Cam, she muttered under her breath, "The life of the beautiful people."

"Hey! Karate girl!" shouted Carla as she stormed into the backyard. "Don't you know this is private property?"

Tina stared hard at Carla and snarled, "Don't you know it's a crime to kidnap airheads?"

"How dare you!" cried Carla as she grabbed a large stick and started swinging it at Tina.

"Hey," said Cam, "did somebody just call me an airhead?"

Assuming the crouching dragon position, Tina leapt up and screamed, "Hiya!" as she chopped the large stick into small pieces of firewood. Carla tried to kick Tina in the head with her 5th Avenue Arlani pumps, but Tina was too fast for her. Tina countered with a stinging flurry of butterfly slaps, but Carla slipped out of range and Tina only managed to knock some mascara into Carla's eye.

"You brute!" yelled Carla. "You win this time!" She retreated into her fabulous garage, rubbing her one eye. Moments later, she sped from her home in her new super-deluxe toy sports car, but not before she warned Tina. "You'll pay for this, karate girl, you'll pay."

As Tina and Carla finished their battle, Suzy burst through the backdoor of the house. "Oh, my poor Cam!" cried Suzy. "You look at least two pounds fatter than when I last saw you."

"I know," said Cam, "and my skin has been without sunblock now for three hours."

"That vicious woman," said Suzy as she quickly applied some sunblock to his face. "I'll never let you out of my sight again." And then the beautiful couple pressed their perfectly shaped lips together for that perfect postcard kiss and started walking off into the sunset.

"Just a minute," said the librarian doll wagging her finger, "not so fast."

Somewhat annoyed that the librarian doll had ruined her classic exit strategy, Suzy turned around and snapped, "What?"

"You still owe me a book reading, deary."

"But that was back then, when I didn't have my precious Cam."

The librarian doll continued. "I would hate to see Cam involved in another kidnapping episode in the near future."

Suzy's eyes widened. "It was you all along, wasn't it?"

The librarian doll grinned. "Come along, Suzy, *Green Eggs and Ham* awaits you." And it was on that day that Suzy read her first book. After that, she was never the same.

Super Duper Noodle Poodle

In a universe parallel to our own, there once was a soupy star cluster known as the Great Ladle. And at the end of that ladle lay a hot, noodley world called Noodleland.

Noodleland was a world much like Earth. The macaroni tribe lived at the east end, the elbow noodles to the south, and the spaghetti noodles in the middle. There was a mayor, a police chief, some noodle physicians and, of course, a large number of noodle poodles. And because the noodle people loved their bendy shape so much, houses, trees and roads were also made out of oodles and oodles of noodles.

But Noodleland was also a world that was very different than Earth. The roots of plants sat in tin cans and the sky had a lid that the Noodle people would close at night. When it rained, it rained upwards, and the rocks were made out of salt and pepper. Sometimes, little fairies would come by and dust all the flowers with Parmesan cheese.

The one thing that the Noodlians feared was dryness. When there was a lack of moisture in the air, Noodle people shaking hands would often find themselves stuck in a twisted bundle. Others got glued to their chairs or were simply left stuck to their bed in a twisted, noodley clump. To avoid these catastrophes, the noodle people spent the majority of their day in water, and the sun was allowed in their tin can world for only five hours a day.

The Noodlians shared their planet with another group of creatures called the Mighty Meatball Men. Like the Noodle people, they too had a mayor, a police chief, some meatball physicians and many meatball mutts. And because the meatball people loved their firm round shape so much, all of their houses, trees and roads were made out of mounds and mounds of meatball-like circles.

Unlike the Noodle people, however, the Mighty Meatball Men did not enjoy hot rainstorms. Being made primarily out of meat, they preferred the hotter and slightly dryer climate of the volcano tunnels. All day long they would roll from one end of the tunnels to the other playing pass the garlic or hide and go beef. Occasionally, they would swim in the hot red volcano sauce spiced with assorted seasonings.

For many centuries, the two societies lived peacefully on the same tin-can planet. The noodle people would slither down squishy noodle sidewalks, jump into hot pots of water and pray to their Noodle God. The meatball men would roll around underground, spray each other with hot tomato sauce and pray to their Meatball God.

This all ended one morning, however, when Mergooklius, king of the Mighty Meatball Men of Mount Speguvious, awoke with a strange vision. Summoning all of his subjects to the central chamber of the volcano, he rolled in a giant circle and shared his vision with his loyal subjects.

"I, King Mergooklius, have had a vision." Everyone fell silent and rolled around in tiny circles of anticipation. "The writings of the ancients," continued Mergooklius, "have shown me our destiny. A path of superiority and destruction."

All the meatball men gasped. "What do you mean, Sire?"

"The Noodle people are different than us. Therefore, we must destroy their civilization." At first, the Mighty Meatball Men were silent. As far as they were concerned, Noodle people were little squiggly creatures that no one had ever wanted to harm. And yet, it was the decree of their king, and it was a vision, and there was no doubt that their Meatball God must have made him king for a reason. They pondered and talked, and talked and pondered, and consulted their mushroom oracle, and eventually all the Meatball Men agreed with their king's decree. The Noodle people were different and therefore needed to be destroyed.

Four days later, Mergooklius had gathered his barbarian tribe of Meatball Warriors from Mount Speguvious. Mergooklius's plan was simple: a direct full frontal meatball and hot lava sauce assault. Four of his Meatball Warriors would stay behind and stoke the volcano so that hot searing tomato sauce could be poured onto the Noodle people. The rest of the Meatball Warriors would march forward, carrying giant forks and spoons to spear and swirl their enemy. King Mergooklius himself would be catapulted off Mount Speguvious into the middle of the steamy noodleworld. The plan seemed perfect; victory would be theirs. The Meatball army began to advance as soon as they saw their fearless king being flung into the jaws of war.

"I want to speak to the mayor," roared Mergooklius as he splatted into the middle of Noodleland's City Hall. The thin noodle walls wobbled.

"I'm the mayor," said an old, fragile noodle as he slithered toward the juicy visitor. "Is there something I can help you with?" he asked.

"I am Mergooklius, king of the Mighty Meatball Men of Mount Speguvious," announced the giant meatball. Then, he made a giant circle to demonstrate how powerful he was.

"Mergooklius, Mergooklius . . . " The mayor thumbed through his appointment book. "I don't seem to have you listed anywhere. Are you sure you had an appointment?" King Mergooklius began bouncing up and down, splattering red-hot sauce everywhere and bending the rubbery noodle floor to the point where it nearly collapsed. "But I suppose I could squeeze you in," added the mayor hastily.

"We are offended by your noodle-like ways," shouted Mergooklius, his stinky garlic and tomato meatball breath filling the entire room, "therefore, prepare to be invaded."

The Noodle mayor stood silent in disbelief as Mergooklius stormed out of his office. What could his people have possibly said or done to make the Mighty Meatball men so angry? As the Noodle mayor thought about the idea of invasion further, he called forth his thin stringy army. There were about 80 of them, and only half were straight enough to stand upright. Watching the floppy soldiers slowly slither to their battle stations, the Noodle mayor was filled with dread. "Heavens to lasagne," he murmured to himself, "we're going to be massacred."

Fortunately, a massacre did not take place that day. For even as wicked people abound, there is always a hero in the midst of wickedness, a person or animal or creature willing to stand up against the mighty meatballs of this world and remain true to their inner noodleliness. And so it was with Super Noodle Poodle and his sidekick, Pasta Puppy.

It was about 4:15 in the afternoon on the Plains of Ravioli. The Mighty Meatball Men had speared a number of Noodle people, who were being dragged back to the hot, searing lava of Mount Speguvious in garlic chains. Pasta Puppy, just having returned from the library, saw what was taking place and tried to save the Noodle people by using his wiggly teeth to bite the arms of the mighty meatball men. Unfortunately, they bounced off the muscular meatball arms, and soon Pasta Puppy was put into onion ring handcuffs and dragged off with the rest of the Noodlians. Using his paw to switch on the global positioning device on his collar, Pasta Puppy attempted to alert Super Noodle Poodle of his whereabouts. He hoped that being underground would not block the signal.

Far above the volcano world, Super Noodle Poodle was testing out toilet water. "Hey, not bad. Minty fresh!" he said as he wiggled over to the next toilet. It was then that Super Noodle Poodle noticed the blinking light. Inspecting the wristwatch on his noodle paw a little closer, Super Noodle Poodle determined the exact location of his partner. "Why is Pasta Puppy in Volcano Land?" he wondered. But before Super Noodle Poodle could think about this situation any further, a Giant Meatball Warrior burst into the room and ladled him with a soup strainer.

"What seems to be the problem?" said Super Noodle Poodle.

"We have been given orders that you are our enemy," declared the Meatball man. The Meatball Warrior proceeded to shove Super Noodle Poodle down a hole with a wooden spoon.

"Enemy?" barked Super Noodle Poodle as he felt himself falling through several layers of sedimentary noodles and landing on a hot red tomato covered in parsley. He had always thought that the two cultures were friends. But when 10 bite-sized Meatball Warriors seized him, stuffed him into a giant onion and rolled him toward the scalding tomato lava, he began to think that perhaps he had been mistaken.

Soon Super Noodle Poodle was at the edge of the volcano, once more reunited with his faithful sidekick, both facing peril in the only way they knew how—courageously.

With his tail at half-mast, Pasta Puppy turned to his friend and said, "Well, if we're going to die, at least we are going to die together."

Super Noodle Poodle licked his friend's face, partly to comfort him, partly to taste the delicious seasonings that were stuck to Pasta Puppy's forehead. Escape would be difficult, as there were no noodle-sized holes or oregano ropes to slither down on. Although the guards had released Super Noodle Poodle from the giant onion, his body had lost a lot of water from all the crying caused by the onion rings. The searing heat of the volcano world made things worse, as their skin was drying out and beginning to crack.

"If only I could get that giant onion out of my pores," cried Super Noodle Poodle.

"Do you think we'll be thrown in next?" asked Pasta Puppy anxiously.

"That is a distinct possibility, Pasta Puppy."

Super Noodle Poodle looked grimly at the large number of Meatball Men who were currently floating in the lava. The situation seemed hopeless. But Super Noodle Poodle had gotten out of situations more hopeless than this before. Perhaps if the guards were all floating in a straight line, and perhaps if he and Pasta Puppy were quick enough, perhaps they could bounce on them and get to the other side of the volcano. But then from the deep recesses of his noodle mind, Super Noodle Poodle thought of an even better plan. Pointing toward the round markings on the wall of the volcano, he asked the meatball guards, "Hey, Beefy Boy, do you know who wrote those?"

One of the Meatball guards looked at what Super Noodle Poodle's brittle, onion-covered paw was pointing at. "You slimy Noodlian, how dare you look at the sacred writings of the old ones."

Super Noodle Poodle shook his head. "Oh dear, the old ones certainly aren't going to be pleased."

"What are you talking about?" demanded the guard.

Super Noodle Poodle arched an eyebrow. "You fool, it's as plain as macaroni and cheese. That lettering is obviously written in Spaghettios, and you are ignoring the commandments of your elders," said Super Noodle Poodle.

The guard was stunned. There had always been much speculation regarding the ancient writings in the meatball community, but no meatball man in history had ever been able to decode the strange noodle-like letters.

Suddenly, the entire volcano chamber began to shake. "What's going on here," boomed a loud voice. It was none other than King Mergooklius himself.

"I was just saying to one of your underlings that I can translate that ancient inscription there," said Super Noodle Poodle.

King Mergooklius folded his arms across his meaty chest and said scornfully, "You, a mere noodle pooch, read the wisdom of the old ones? I highly doubt that."

"That's Noodle Poodle," asserted Super Noodle Poodle. "And yes, I happen to know what it says." He then turned his back on the king and added, "But I don't know if I want to tell you now."

The King demanded, "Speak, you noodle varmint, what does it say?"

"No, I don't feel like it," said the clever Noodle Poodle.

"We have ways to make you talk, pooch." King Mergooklius then spun round in a circle and ordered, "Guard, fetch me a cheese grater."

As Mergooklius turned to speak to the guard, Super Noodle Poodle winked at Pasta Puppy, who immediately knew what to do. Pasta Puppy began to whimper and pretend that he was overcome with fear. "Please, Super Noodle Poodle, just tell him," Pasta Puppy yelped. "Tell him for my sake."

"Fear not, my trusty companion. I will not allow them to torment you," said Super Noodle Poodle. He then turned to face Mergooklius and said, "You win."

The king smiled.

Super Noodle Poodle put on his glasses and carefully translated the ancient writings aloud. "Recipe for a good planet. First, we must consider the Noodle people as our friends and learn to live in harmony."

"Friends? Harmony?"   King Mergooklius was astonished. He was so sure that his vision had been right.

Looking at Super Noodle suspiciously, he said, "How do I know that you aren't trying to trick me?"

Super Noodle Poodle thrust his collar forward. "Hey, if you don't believe me, why don't you check out this universal translator of ancient languages?"

King Mergooklius removed some of the onionskin that still covered Super Noodle Poodle's body and typed in the words, only to find that the pooch was correct. King Mergooklius stood in shocked silence for several painful moments, wondering how he could have gotten everything so wrong. Finally, he turned to his subjects and announced humbly, "Everyone, I have a new vision."

All the mighty meatball men gasped, "What is it, Sire?"

"The writings of the ancients have given me a new vision of friendship and harmony. Therefore, we shall not cook any more Noodle people; rather, we will apologize and make amends for this unfortunate recent course of action."

The Meatball Men fell silent. As far as they were concerned, the Noodlians were sneaky, untrustworthy creatures who were now their enemy. And besides, many of the Meatball Men enjoyed the excitement of preparing for more battles and destruction. Yet, they all had to admit, it was the decree of their king, and it was a vision, and there was no doubt that their Meatball God must have made him king for a reason. They pondered and talked, and talked and pondered, and consulted their mushroom oracle once again. Eventually all the

Meatball Men agreed with their king's decree and they promised to play friendly. The Noodle people really were like themselves, and they deserved to be saved.

That day, the Mighty Meatball Men and the Noodlians became friends, and they all lived happily every after on their swirling little tin-can planet, or at least happily ever after until they ran into the Crazy Purple Monkey Men of Nylar Seven, but that is, of course, another story.

Greta and the Cheese Noodle

Greta was a good girl in many ways. She did her homework. She was nice to her teachers. She even helped her father with the dishes. But Greta also had a dark side. She loved eating cheese noodles.

Every breakfast, lunch and supper, Greta would eat cheese noodles with her meal. Sometimes she slipped cheese noodles under the cheese of her cheeseburger. Sometimes she crushed cheese noodles into her milk when her father wasn't looking. Sometimes she hid cheese noodles in her ice cream. At night, she would leave cheese noodles under her pillow so that she might dream about their heavenly cheesy aroma while she slept.

"Greta," scolded her father one morning at the breakfast table, "have you been eating those delicious cheese noodles again?"

"No, Papa," said Greta as she wiped orange crumbs from her lips.

Seizing Greta's clenched fist, her father opened her hand and demanded, "What do you call these?"

Greta glanced at the squashed cheese noodle evidence of her early morning feeding frenzy. "Those are," Greta looked up at the ceiling, "I don't know, Papa."

Her father rolled his eyes as he reached behind the table and swung open her lunch box, "And these?"

Greta tried to think of an excuse, but when she saw her entire lunch box overflowing with cheese noodles, her mind went blank. She was overcome by the smell of cheesy goodness. "It's a mystery how those got in there, Papa" she said.

"Greta," sighed her father, "if I've told you once, I've told you a thousand times: cheese noodles are for snacks and for snacks only." Putting his hands on his hips, he added sternly, "If you can not put an end to this cheese noodle eating of yours, I certainly will."

"Yes, Papa," said Greta.

Greta tried to do as her father asked, but the lure of the cheese noodle proved to be too strong, and soon Greta found herself gorging once again. Forking out money for bag after bag after bag of cheese noodles, Greta desperately sought a way to break her habit. She tried switching to other brands, whole wheat and sardine–flavoured cheese noodles, goose liver cheese noodles, spinach and horse radish–flavoured cheese noodles, curried earthworm cheese noodles, but still she wanted more. Feeling that she needed some help to quit, she went to a cheese noodle hypnotist.

"You hate cheese noodles, Greta," her hypnotist would say, "but you love paying me money to help slowly cure you."

After spending several more dollars in several more therapy sessions, Greta believed she was finally cured. This, however, was before the fateful morning when her father caught her orange-handed in the bathroom.

"Greta!" his yell an equal portion of shock and disappointment, "you told me you had quit!"

"I thought I had too, Papa," said Greta guiltily, her eyes underlined with dark circles. She had been up the entire night stuffing herself with the tasty but forbidden snack treats.

Greta's father snatched the cheese noodle bag out of Greta's hands. "From now on, I'm going to have to keep a more watchful eye on your eating habits," he said.

And so Greta's home became a prison. Her father searched through her pockets before every meal. He checked every meal for clever cheese noodle camouflage. He combed through her macaroni and cheese to see if there was any suspicious looking extra noodle activity. He tasted her orange juice to see if there were any suspicious crunchy cheesy bits.

But this did not stop Greta. Instead of hiding cheese noodles in her food, she merely stuffed them into her ears, her nose and, occasionally, her bellybutton. She then ate them when her father was not around. Sometimes, she even stuck a few cheese noodles between her toes and made cheese noodle toe jam, which she later spread on toast. Truly, Greta had become a hardcore chain cheese-noodler, reaching for a fresh cheese noodle even before she had finished crunching the last.

At school, Greta's teacher became concerned when she saw a trail of orange dust follow Greta wherever she went. Tasting a few of the crumbs, Greta's teacher concluded that it was a dangerous cheesy snack treat and decided to pay her father a visit.

"I've tried to stop her," pleaded Greta's father guiltily, "but she just seems to find ways of smuggling the cheese noodles into school anyway."

Greta's teacher nodded as she glanced at the tiny piles of cheese noodle powder sitting on the kitchen table. "Yes, Greta is a clever girl. I hate to say this, but it looks as though your daughter's cheese noodle disorder is spiralling out of control."

"But what can we do?" said her father helplessly.

Greta's teacher drummed her fingers on the table. After a long silence, she said, "I think, at this point, we must take drastic measures. If you sign this permission form, I'll handle all the details."

One week later, Greta was enrolled in a special "Carrots and Broccoli School" so that she, like other students before her, could be "re-veg-ucated." Every morning, the children pledged allegiance to the broccoli flag and then sang the carrot anthem. After they finished tending a vegetable plot in the back of the school, they came in, sat in their lettuce-shaped desks and took out pencils that were made out of pressed rhubarb.

"Now," said her new teacher, "when we eat a tomato right from our garden, there's no sugar or salt added. What type of snack do we call that?"

The children robotically replied, "Natural."

"Very good, my clever bunch of turnips," said the teacher as she took out her zucchini chalk holder and wrote on the board "natural = good." She turned back to her class. "Yesterday, we read a book about an evil chocolate cheesecake monster who tried to kill Charlie the Cheerful Carrot and his sad companion, Lucy the Lonely Lettuce."

Upon hearing the word cheesecake, most of the students frowned and started to talk among themselves about the dangers of fatty foods. But when Greta heard the word "cheese," she began to smile. It reminded her that she still had one precious cheese noodle hidden in the depths of her left nostril. She decided that this would be the perfect time to enjoy one last forbidden snack. She pulled the cheese noodle out of her nose, but before she could bite into the moist and soggy but still delicious noodle, a very loud alarm bell went off.

"Snack alert, snack alert," said a mechanical voice from the speakers on the wall.

Greta quickly popped her tasty cheese noodle in her mouth while there was still time.

"Somebody will pay for this," said the teacher angrily as she walked up and down the aisles. "Confess now and things will go easier for you later."

The children stayed silent in their seats, each one of them trying to look as vegetable-like as possible. As the teacher's eyes continued to search the room, Greta noticed a bit of cheese dust that lay on the floor.

"Oh yes," said the teacher, filling her nostrils with air, "I can almost smell the culprit now."

Greta tried to cover the cheese powder with her shoe, but to no avail. Sensing she would be caught at any second, she shot out of her desk and made a dash for the door.

"Not so fast," said the teacher as she latched on to one of Greta's braids. "Let me see your tongue."

Greta stuck out her tongue reluctantly. It was orange.

The teacher nodded as she summoned three white-coated men to take Greta away. Within minutes they were dragging Greta away before her behaviour could undermine the other children's progress.

"Where are you taking me?!" demanded Greta.

"The vegetable dungeon," said a big burly man with cauliflower-coloured hair. The men led Greta into the vegetable garden behind the school. They put Greta into the middle of a genetically engineered giant cucumber and told her that her only escape was to eat her way out. She tried to crawl up to the small hatch at the top of the enormous cucumber, but it was sealed shut. They were right. There was only one way out.

They say it took her a week to gnaw her way to freedom. They say a week in that giant cucumber cured Greta of her desire for eating cheese noodles.

And they were right, it did. As Greta chewed through the last bit of cucumber and made her way to freedom, she realized that she no longer needed cheese noodles to feel happy. Her cheese noodle addiction had just gotten her into more and more trouble, and her life had been, when she thought about it, just one giant pickle of a mess. She realized she could pass on her wisdom to thousands of other children who had lost control over their own nutritional habits.

She decided to write a book that would help others. She called it *Escaping Your Giant Pickle* and it was noted as being the most inspiring self-help book written in a decade by critics far and wide. Greta was destined to make the world a healthier place, and nothing was going to stop her, not even the legal battle sparked by teachers at the Carrots and Broccoli School who decided to sue her for the rights to her bestselling book.

The Gerboopadoop

The sun shone brightly that day in Derby. The animals in the soda saloon were fanning themselves with their pink soda napkins, and Erma the Emu took the last sip of her Sleety Joe chocolate shake.

"Well, I best be heading off," she said as she tossed a couple of coins at the soda saloon bartender.

"Where you headed, girl?" asked the soda master.

Erma spun her empty glass around in a circle. "The desert. I'm going to find me a gerboopadoop."

A sudden silence fell over the bar.

"I heard those things were extinct," said a kangaroo sitting at a nearby barstool.

"I heard they're worth a million dollars," said his koala friend.

The soda saloon bartender picked up Erma's glass and began wiping it clean. "Well, if you ask me," he said quietly, "those things are nothing but trouble." Then he put the glass gently down on the table and said to Erma firmly, "Do yourself a favour, girl. Leave it alone."

Erma smirked at the bartender, swung her rucksack on her back and headed for the exit. "Save me a Sleety Joe," she said, and then swung the door shut.

Erma left Derby that day at high noon. Equipped with only a map, some traps and, for some reason, a few Himalayan gnats, she plotted her way through various stockmen camps en route. Other than avoiding a few crocodiles, she figured that the trip would be short and sweet.

But the trek was anything but short, and the places she visited anything but sweet. In her first stockmen camp, the women chewed dried prunes, and the men let them. The second camp was even rougher than the first: the women were tougher and the prunes were even drier. Wild fights erupted over the sale of Girl Scout cookies. Old stockwomen carried purse-sized horsewhips and knew how to use them. Determined not to let the old ladies get to her, Erma shook the dried prunes off her feet and walked on.

After visiting a few more prune-ridden towns, it became apparent that Erma was not alone. Someone or something was following her. Turning sharply, she called out to the darkness, "Is someone there?"

A small carpet snake, the second least poisonous snake in the world, presented itself.

"What do you want?" asked Erma harshly.

For a few seconds, the snake just made hissing sounds and thought about his dirty laundry. Then, frustrated by boredom, he slithered up to the enormous bird and said in an oily voice, "I heard you talking to that man in the soda saloon back there in Derby and thought you might need a friend."

Erma backed away from the snake. "I don't need any more friends," she said.

"Ah yes," said the snake as he pushed his way past the determined emu, "but do you have a friend that can do this?" The snake flattened itself on the ground, making the shape of a large arrow.

"What are you doing?" asked Erma.

"You see, blondie," said the snake as he picked up one of her fallen blond outer feathers with his tail, "I can show you the way to your precious gerboopadoop."

"I have a map," she snapped.

The snake blew the feather away. "Sure you have a map, blondie, but there's no compass on the map, is there?"

Erma reached into her rucksack, only to find out that the snake was correct. Without a compass, there was no way of telling which way to go.

"You could find the gerboopadoop yourself," continued the snake smugly. "After all, what does it matter if you spend your entire youth looking for this thing? I think you will look nice as an old bushwoman."

Erma thought about the snake's offer. Certainly, she didn't trust him, but she also didn't like the idea of spending the next 10 or 20 years in the dry, wrinkle-producing desert either. "Alright," said Erma, "but no tricks."

The snake wiggled its tongue excitedly, as certain types of animals will do from time to time when they're excited. "Now if you'll just hand over that map."

Erma pecked the snake's tail away with her beak. "Nice try, snakey, but nobody touches this map. I show you the map, and you point the way."

The snake agreed. And so, much like the dance of two scorpions, the snake and the emu began a distrustful journey together, each saying only as much as the other needed to know.

Meanwhile, in a soda saloon not too far away, a kangaroo, a wallaby, a platypus and a polar bear were playing a game of Texas hold 'em. The group had been playing for several hours, and the wallaby, now short stacked with only a few chips left and desperate, was ready to go all in.

"Call," said the platypus to the wallaby as he gleefully glanced at his cards.

The wallaby stared doubtfully at the platypus. "You can't possibly have two aces".

"Why not?" said the platypus.

"Because I have three aces!" said the wallaby

The platypus grinned. "Yes, but I got mine first."

"Listen, you," said the wallaby as he reached across the table and grabbed the platypus by the throat, "either you tell me where your extra ace came from, or this soda pop goes all over your nice clean shirt."

At that moment, a quiet hush fell over the soda saloon. The kangaroo began to reach for his raincoat. The polar bear had other things on his mind.

"Let him go," warned the polar bear.

The wallaby looked up at the polar bear's teeth, which were sharp and certainly unbrushed. One chomp from those teeth could lead to serious infection and possibly even a case of the outback jiggles. Not wanting to anger the bear further, he unhanded the platypus and stomped off.

"Thanks for saving me bacon, mate," said the much-relieved platypus as he stuck his webbed foot on the polar bear's shoulder.

"You're no mate of mine," said the polar bear coldly as he locked eyes with the platypus. The one half of his face sneered with pleasure, the other half drooped with disappointment. "Word has it that you had a visit by an emu named Erma."

"Yes, I did," replied the platypus. "Seems like she was looking for the gerboopadoop. I'd like to help you more, but you know," the platypus paused for second and then said with a sly smile, "my memory isn't quite what it used to be."

"Maybe this will help refresh your memory," said the bear as he grabbed the platypus by the scruff the neck, ready to biff him in the nose.

"Oh yes, of course," said the platypus, "it's all coming back to me; they were on their way to the mangroves. Left here a couple of hours ago."

The polar bear turned to his friend, the camel, who stood waiting by the exit. "Looks like we found them," said the polar bear as he got up and swaggered toward the door. And so the polar bear and the camel went on tracking Erma the emu. They knew it was now only a matter of time.

A new day had dawned, and the snake had accidentally led Erma into the middle of a particularly stinky swamp. In the dank undergrowth of the mangroves, there were many nasty animals, including crocodiles, lizards and even one or two vicious aardvarks (which is very strange considering that aardvarks do not usually live in Australia). Tired from their earlier battle with the aardvarks that day, and having finally escaped the clutches of the stinky swamp, the two travelers decided to take a rest in a tree beneath the setting sun.

"Knock knock," said the snake.

"Who's there?" said Erma.

The snake smiled. "Sorry, it slipped my mind."

Erma slid her swagman hat over her eyes and leaned back on the tree. "That's low, even for you, mate."

The snake merely laughed.

"By the way," said Erma, "you know that last batch of stew we ate? I think it was one of your relatives."

The snake sat bolt upright.

"Goodnight snake," said Erma as she grinned and rolled over onto her side

And so it was that Erma and the snake's fledgling distrust for one another grew into a deep and profound suspicion. Neither animal was willing to tell the other a joke ever again.

The bitter memory of the mangrove mudflats were soon swept away by hot winds and sand the next day. Erma and the snake traveled side by side, she with her slow, dinosaur-like strides, and he with his quick, small slithers. While the two shadows trudged onward through the never-ending wasteland, a wedge tail eagle flew mockingly high over head.

By high noon, the desert had become a dry sauna. The two animals began to sizzle, the dust in the air cutting their throats like tiny daggers. Stopping for a few seconds to catch their breath, the snake shed its skin and the emu shook some of the gritty, orange sand off her feathers.

"It sure is hot, blondie," remarked the snake. "You sure you aren't getting tired?"

Erma smiled. "Just awake enough to see that you never get this map, snake." Tilting her head skyward, she added, "We'd better find some sort of shelter before nightfall." The snake agreed.

Erma slept uneasily that night, her dreams haunted by the tortured cries of a gerboopadoop. Why was she so intent on finding it? Was it to become famous? Was it to become rich? Or was it neither? Was it just something she had to do? As these questions continued to plague her sleep, Erma woke up squawking, her feathers soaked with sweat.

"So we meet again," said an eerie voice in the dark.

Erma jerked upright and narrowed her eyes. It was the polar bear. Dressed in a black vest and a red bow tie, the polar bear looked every bit like the no-gooder she knew he was.

"What are you doing here?" asked Erma.

The polar bear took out a fire ant cream puff, sliced off a piece and slowly began to eat it. "I hear you're hunting gerboopadoops."

Lying back down in her sleeping bag, Erma said flatly, "Well, you heard wrong."

"Oh really," said the polar bear, his eyes sparkling like ice. "I also heard that you were running low on food."

Staring at the cream puff with oven-sized eyes, Erma tried to hold back a growl that came from her belly. She knew that the polar bear was right. There was probably only one day's worth of food supplies left, two days at the most.

"The camel here is carrying enough food to get all four of us to our destination. But if you'd rather starve . . . " The polar bear's voice trailed off.

"Hey, is that food I see before my eyes?" said the snake as he poked his head up out of the sand.

The polar bear grinned, reached into his rucksack and tossed the snake a fire ant cream puff.

"I don't trust you," said Erma.

"Well, I trust him," said the snake as he gobbled down the cream puff whole. "It wasn't poisoned, was it?""

The polar bear took out another cream puff and ate it slowly in front of the snake.

"See, blondie," the snake said with a laugh, "I told you we could trust him."

Erma looked away.

"So," said the snake to the polar bear, "what's a nice guy like you doing in a hot place like this anyway?"

The polar bear licked off the blade of his knife and stuck it back into his vest pocket. "I like to come here to get out of the cold."

"You're weird," replied the snake. Seeing the polar bear bare his teeth, the snake added quickly, "but weird in a good way."

"We'll sleep here tonight and set up the traps tomorrow," announced the polar bear.

"Yes, of course, sleep, what a wonderful idea," said the snake, his tongue beginning to dart back and forth. "I'll keep watch while everyone else rests."

The polar bear's eyes turned white as icebergs. "I'd rather stick cactus in my ears," he snarled.

Erma, equally distrustful of the polar bear, chimed in, "I suppose its every animal for itself."

And so the four animals stayed up all night, each of their eyes locked on each other. This standoff went on for several days as the unlikely band of adventurers journeyed forth. At last, in the heat of a particularly punishing afternoon, Erma looked down at the painful blisters on her feet and said, "I think I'm getting really sunburnt."

"Only sunburnt?" complained the snake. "Try having your back stepped on by a polar bear."

The polar bear grunted. "Well, I've got a toothache. That's far more horrible than either a sunburn or being stepped on."

As Erma, the snake and the polar bear kept grumbling over which one of them had it the worst, the camel, an animal of few words, finally broke his silence. "Then give it up," he said.

The other three animals immediately stopped arguing. "Give up the hunt?" said the polar bear incredulously. "After all we've been through?"

"We can't possibly give up now," hissed the snake.

Erma shook her head. "The camel's right. We've been out here for days now, and we've seen nothing."

"But we haven't got to the right spot yet," argued the snake.

Erma stared hard at her twisty business partner. "Okay snake," she said sarcastically, "what is the right spot? Over there? Over here? A few feet to the left? You're the compass, how do I even know that your sense of direction is right?"

"There you go again, blondie, always doubting me," hissed the snake. "You haven't thanked me once."

"Here you go then. Thanks for nothing," Erma the Emu replied, "and stop calling me 'blondie.'"

The polar bear tried to interject, but Erma was on a roll.

"And the food," said Erma as she kicked an empty container into the air. "Well, that was just one more thing that didn't work out."

"Are you suggesting that's my fault?" asked the polar bear coldly.

Erma lowered her eyes. "No, it's nobody's fault," she said. With her eyes scanning the vast turquoise horizon before her, she added in an empty and distant voice, "You know what? Maybe those archaeologists were right. Maybe the gerboopadoop is extinct, or better yet, maybe it never existed at all."

The other three animals gasped as though Erma had said the unthinkable.

"Of course it exists," protested the polar bear.

"Then what does it look like?" asked Erma.

The polar bear scratched his head. "I don't know."

"Exactly," said Erma as she began gathering her things. "I'm leaving."

"But what about us?" said the snake.

Erma reached into her knapsack and threw her map to the snake. "Here, may you enjoy the rest of your life in the desert."

Watching Erma's burnt feet slowly carry her over the nearest sand dune, the three remaining animals stood motionless, as though they had been stung by a particularly angry mud wasp.

"Perhaps the emu has a point," said the polar bear dejectedly.

"I'm kind of tired of this whole thing anyway," hissed the snake.

The camel, an animal of few words, just nodded his head.

And so as the sun set that day, the four animals went their separate ways. The desert was once again emptied of its visitors, and the wind ever so softly carried the faintest laughter of the mysterious and not-quite-extinct gerboopadoop.

Le Papier Prince

(The Paper Prince)

Martha didn't know for how long she had loved him. It seemed like five years, but it was probably more. She saw his face wherever she went: in supermarkets, in bookstores, on television, in video games. Everywhere she looked, he was there.

His face was like any movie star's. He had long, grey ears and a skinny, furry body. When he smiled with his big buckteeth, every flashbulb in the world seemed ready to light up. His name was Brad Rabbitt. Millions loved him, but none more than Martha. She thought that "Brad" was the most beautiful name in the whole world, and she would listen for it everywhere she went. Before she fell asleep, she said goodnight to Brad Rabbitt, wherever he might be, and when she woke, he was always the first thing on her mind.

And so it came to pass that Martha began to live a life with him. Every morning, she would get up and eat breakfast with him. When she read about one his new crazy adventures, she would shake her head and say to the picture on the magazine before her, "Silly Rabbitt, tricks are for kids." After breakfast, she would complete her morning ritual by gently tucking him into her knapsack and taking him to school. There, she would talk about his life with all her friends.

"I thought his last movie was awful," complained one of her classmates. "His fur's lost its sheen. His hops are so wooden. His nose twitching's lost its sparkle."

Martha gave her classmate the best withering look she could muster. "I thought he was wonderful," she said with quiet rage in her voice. Then she spat, "Who cares what you think, anyway. You're not fit to polish his paws."

Slightly startled by Martha's outburst, the classmate leant over the table and sang with a half-smirking voice, "You love Brad. You love Brad"

Martha picked up her magazine protectively and held it close. "No," she blurted, "I don't. I just appreciate his talent."

"Oh, really?" said the classmate as she took another sip of her slightly sour milk. "You know," she said coolly, "he's never going to marry you."

Martha's lips drooped like two limp inchworms. "You think I don't know that?" she snarled.

"So why are you always talking about him?"

Martha turned back to her classmate and said, "I find him furry and entertaining, that's all." Then she grabbed her magazine and ran all the way home.

Though people tried to convince Martha of her foolishness in loving a paper prince, Martha would not stop. She continued to see all of Brad Rabbitt's movies and buy all of his DVDs. She read every gossip column and wrote, on average, two letters to him every day, every one of them unanswered. She put herself on the Brad Rabbitt diet, a strict diet of carrots, onions and peas. She even bought a pair of his dirty socks that were being sold on Tree-Bay for $250.

One day, a strange wind rose from the west. Martha's class was coming in from recess, and just inside the door, as they were entering the hallway, the wind blew in with them, bringing all sorts of paper scraps from outside. At first, there was just a light flapping of pages, but soon the wind blew in a frenzy. Paper began to whip around in circles, as if the hallway had been transformed into a giant dryer.

"What's happening?" said Martha's teacher as he tried to get the children into his class for a math test. The paper swirled faster, until at last, it took the form of a large rabbit.

Martha gasped. "It's him," she cried as a large bucktoothed smile began to emerge out of the swirling paper sculpture. "It's Brad Rabbitt!"

All the students were stunned into silence. How many saw the same rabbit that day is anybody's guess. "I knew you would come for me," said Martha.

The large rabbit held a fixed paper smile on his face like it was pasted on. It seemed to reach out to Martha with open arms. Martha ran to him as everyone watched as if she ran in slow motion. When Martha began to hug him, his smile fell off.

"Oh my goodness," said Martha. "I'll get you some glue." But before Martha could even turn and begin her search for the precious glue, Brad Rabbitt's long ears fell off, followed by his fluffy tail.

Martha began to panic. There was no time to get any glue. She tried to hold the pieces together with her bare hands, but more of them started to fall off and blow away. "Don't worry, Brad," she said reassuringly. "I'll get you fixed up in no time." But Martha was fooling no one. Panic turned to dread, and dread turned to horror. Neither Martha nor the king's horses nor all the king's men could put Brad Rabbitt back together again. More and more of Brad Rabbitt's body was torn off and blown out the door into the vastness beyond, until at last, he disappeared completely into the wind as though he had never existed at all.

The class stood motionless for several seconds. On the cheek of one of those children, a single tear existed momentarily before being brushed aside. As the last tiny shred of paper blew away into the clouds like a lost snowflake, one of the children left the crowd, came over and put her arm around Martha.

"I'm sorry," she said gently.

Martha said nothing. There was nothing to say.

"You know," the girl added, "he was only a paper prince."

Martha looked into the girl's caring face. After a few seconds, which seemed much longer to anyone watching, Martha spoke in a voice that could not entirely hide the sadness she felt, "You're right, of course. But for a few brief seconds, he was mine."

Toothless

Near the centre of the earth, there is a place where grasshoppers jump around endlessly, their yellow-flecked wings sparkling in the heat of the Earth's core while stone flies flutter from rock to rock. Below the buzzing of their yellow-flecked wings is a lush patch of red lava grass tipped with diamonds. And below the red lava grass one will find a tiny castle made entirely out of children's teeth. This castle is the luxurious, if not entirely comfortable, dwelling for Edwina E. Tootheria, known by mere mortals as "The Tooth Fairy."

Most people imagine that the Tooth Fairy is tiny and cute and awfully sweet, and while Edwina might at times be cute (she, herself, would insist it was closer to a ravishing beauty than a mere cuteness), she is certainly anything but sweet. She is, however, the only living thing in the universe that can withstand the extreme difference between the Earth's surface and the heat of the Earth's core. This ability allows her to thrive as a hardcore businesswoman who makes her living by wheeling and dealing with humans on the surface and the creatures living far below the Earth's crust. Every day, she gets up, puts on a three-piece pin-stripped business suit and prepares to do business between these two worlds.

Her main source of income comes from selling children's teeth to the lava worms that use the enamel to protect their soft flesh against the searing heat of the Earth's core. Like car wax, the tooth enamel only lasts a certain amount of time before it wears off, so the lava worms are, by nature, repeat customers.

"How much will you give me for 10 teeth?" Edwina would ask a lava worm.

After haggling with the lava worm for a few minutes, they would finally agree upon a fair and reasonable price. Depending on how many children in the world lost their teeth the night before and how many had put them beneath their pillow for easy pick-up, this price would vary from day to day on the local enamel market. Edwina had a knack for locating teeth and then selling them for a profit.

Of course, in the beginning, convincing humans to part with their baby teeth was not easy. Some, like Cleopatra, wanted to make them into necklaces instead of giving them up. Edwina made a deal. The Egyptian queen, and all subsequent tooth providers, would get a 10 per cent fee for each tooth. The Tooth Fairy's business had to branch out all over the world in order to make her plan work, but work it did. After only a few hundred years, it became quite the money-making venture, and it remained very lucrative for centuries.

During the first part of the 21st century, however, something went terribly wrong. For no apparent reason, people all over the world began to doubt the Tooth Fairy's existence, and thus the supply of much-needed teeth dwindled to almost nothing. Human beings were no longer dutifully placing teeth under their children's pillows; rather, many of them were actually just throwing these precious teeth into the garbage. Demand for teeth amongst the lava worms far outstripped supply, and at the Earth's core, tooth prices skyrocketed, causing great panic amongst her loyal customers. Many of the lava worms staged protests and demanded that Edwina fill the demand for protective enamel.

"If you don't come up with at least 300 teeth soon," the lava worms warned, "we'll eat you alive." At some level it was a bit of an empty threat, for without Edwina there would be no enamel at all. The thought of being eaten by a lava worm was still rather distressing for Edwina, so she thought up a wonderfully ingenious plan to acquire a new source of teeth, and this is where our story truly begins.

Sammy Sneed, a rather average-looking boy who attended Lincoln elementary, discovered one Tuesday morning that he had lost his first tooth. "Look, Daddy," he cried, opening his mouth wide for his father to see inside, "I lost a tooth."

"That's nice, dear,' said Sammy's father as he turned the first page of the paper. Sammy's father liked reading the paper.

"I'm going to put it under my pillow right now," said Sammy. "I bet the Tooth Fairy leaves a whole sack full of money for it."

Sammy's father put down his paper. "Sammy, there's no such thing as the Tooth Fairy. Now go throw that thing out before it smells."

"Yes, Father," said Sammy sadly.

The next day, Sammy came down for his usual bowl of porridge. And as usual, his father was reading the paper. And everything seemed very normal except for one small thing. Sammy had lost the rest of his teeth.

"What happened to your teeth!" exclaimed Sammy's father.

"I don't know," said Sammy, tearfully. "I just woke up this morning and they were gone."

Sammy's father looked at his upset son and tried to calm him down. "Well," said his father in an even voice, "I suppose they're just baby teeth, so they'll grow back. In the meantime, just wear Grandpa's spare dentures to school."

So Sammy went to school and tried his best to talk with his grandfather's dentures in his mouth. Unfortunately, some of the denture cream came loose, and the dentures fell out onto the lap of the girl beside him.

"Ms. Gingivitis," she cried, "Sammy's teeth are biting me!"

Ms. Gingivitis began to scold Sammy. "Sammy, stop biting little—" The teacher stopped when she saw the large black hole that was Sammy's mouth. "Good heavens! Sammy, where are your teeth?"

Everybody's head turned and soon calamity broke out in the class. Shrieks rang through the hallways as word of Sammy's toothlessness spread. It wasn't long before the principal, Mrs. Floss, rushed into the room.

Speaking to the nurse beside her, Mrs. Floss asked, "Any trace of candy poisoning?"

"No, and he's got a toothbrush in his pencil case," the nurse said after taking Sammy's blood pressure. "Looks like the kid's clean."

"Well," said Ms. Gingivitis, "since we don't know what caused Sammy's problem, it must be his parents' fault. From now on, Sammy, your father and mother will be locked up, and you'll be living with me."

So Sammy's father and mother were sent away, and Sammy stayed that night with Ms. Gingivitis. The problem seemed fixed . . . at least so they thought.

The next day was an ordinary as any other. Lenny Crewtop got beaten up at the drinking fountain, Katie Forenski wore a new designer dress and Wally Wisecracker got sent to the office. But there was one small difference that day. Franklin Gumsy and Brian Incisorson came to class with no teeth.

"More children without teeth!" exclaimed Ms. Gingivitis. "It looks like you'll have to live with me too."

It turned out that soon Ms. Gingivitis would have more than she bargained for. Day after day, more children came to school without teeth and more parents were locked up. By the end of the week, half the entire student population was gumming their peanut butter sandwiches and slurping their applesauce through straws. Nothing in Mrs. Floss's principal training manual had prepared her for a school of toothless children.

"Mrs. Floss," complained Ms. Gingivitis, "I've tried telling the students to brush between meals every day, but the students keep losing their teeth."

"Hmmm," Mrs. Floss began drumming her fingers. "We're missing something." Picking up a piece of chalk and turning to the blackboard, she said, "Let's review the facts." She wrote the facts on the board and drew lines between one word and another. She stared at them until the blurry, scribbled mess became crystal clear. "Of course," she said triumphantly. "We've locked up the parents, but maybe the dentists are the real culprits behind this toothless epidemic. Better lock them up too."

"Good idea," said Ms. Gingivitis.

That afternoon, all the children's dentists were taken into custody and thrown into prison with all the children's parents. It may have been slightly outside the law, but these were desperate times.

Of course, the children did not see these events in the same way as adults. Living with Ms. Gingivitis was actually a lot of fun. Some children even took pride in their new gummy appearance.

Ms. Gingivitis, on the other hand, was not happy. She did not know how many more toothless children she could cram into her tiny house. Driving home that night, she kept wondering why the children lost all of their teeth in one night. All of a sudden, Ms. Gingivitis shouted, "Eureka!" She drove straight to Mildred Stowe's house, the only student in her class who had not yet lost her teeth.

"Mrs. Stowe," said Ms. Gingivitis, "I fear your child is in great danger. I fear that tonight she will become toothless."

Mrs. Stowe looked panicked. She was determined to protect her daughter's pearly whites. "Do you know who is taking our children's teeth?"

"Yes, Mrs. Stowe. I have a hunch, but we'll have to gather more evidence. Now, can you tell me what Mildred had for breakfast?"

"Just normal things, I guess," she answered.

"And what might we conclude would be normal for Mildred?" Ms. Gingivitis asked.

"You know, a little breakfast cereal," Mrs. Stowe continued nervously.

"Can you be more specific about the breakfast cereal, please? Tasty Creamy Wheat? Wholesome Cornflake Crispies?"

"I think it was more like Super Sugary Sparkle Charms, with . . . " Mrs. Stowe's voice hesitated. She blushed, then added, "with, some extra sugar sprinkled on top for flavour."

"Mrs. Stowe, you're positive?"

"Yes, yes," Mrs. Stowe began sobbing, "it's all true."

"Then we have no time to waste," cautioned Ms. Gingivitis.

"What can we do?"

"We wait," said Ms. Gingivitis. "Tonight, by Mildred's bed while she sleeps. If my suspicions are correct, it will be a very interesting evening indeed."

It was about 3:07 in the morning. Both Mrs. Stowe and Ms. Gingivitis were very tired. Suddenly, a bright light flew through the window. It was none other than the Tooth Fairy, Edwina in all her glory, carrying her small bag of tooth extracting equipment.

Stunned by the little glowing light that was stomping on Mildred's pillow, Ms. Gingivitis spoke up. "Just as I thought." Edwina was momentarily taken aback by the loud human voice. "Why have you been taking our children's teeth?" demanded Ms. Gingivitis.

"Oh, so one of you finally figured it out," said the Tooth Fairy. "Took you long enough."

"Why are you doing this to the children?" repeated Ms. Gingivitis.

"Two words: revenge and economics," snapped Edwina.

"What?"

"Look, the arrangement with you humans was simple. You leave the teeth. I leave a finder's fee. I dispose of the teeth. I sell the teeth for a small profit. A real win-win situation. Everybody was happy, until this century, when you humans forgot about holding up your end of the bargain."

Ms. Gingivitis was shocked. "What are you talking about?"

"I'm talking money. A girl has to eat, you know, and you humans are taking food off my table every time you throw out a child's tooth instead of leaving it for me," Edwina said angrily.

"And that's why you steal their teeth right out of their mouths?" asked Mrs. Stowe.

"Hey, it's you guys that stopped believing in me. And besides, if I don't restore the flow of tooth enamel, the lava worms are going to eat me," said Edwina.

Ms. Gingivitis was puzzled. "Lava worms?"

"Yes, lava worms," said Edwina. "Have you ever seen a lava worm? Hideous, really. They have these large, pointy teeth, and they drool all the time."

"But the children need their teeth," said Mrs. Stowe.

"Yeah, well so do I," said the Tooth Fairy. She scratched her tiny chin and then added thoughtfully, "I'll tell you what, if you can find me a decent stockpile of, say, 300 baby teeth by tomorrow night, I'll give the children their teeth back."

"Three hundred baby teeth!" exclaimed Ms. Gingivitis.

"Unless . . . " The Tooth Fairy stared at Ms. Gingivitis's large incisors and started glowing with a bright idea.

The next morning, all the kids arrived in class with large, gleaming teeth.

"Look, Ms. Gingivitis. I have my teeth back," yelled Francine.

"I have mine too!" shouted Frank.

The children were so happy. They had their teeth back, and their parents had been released from prison before school that morning. Yet through the cheers of their celebration, there was one person who remained oddly silent.

"Hey, Ms. Gingivitis," said George, "how come you're not saying anything?"

Ms. Gingivitis looked at the children and smiled. "I'm thso happy for you, clath." And she was happy for the children, as happy as each and every one of their now toothless parents.

Mr. Red and Mr. Green

Twenty-nine years had slipped past and in all that time Mr. Red had been a model teacher. He had stood in front of the same chalkboard using the same brand of chalk to unravel the mysteries of the world to generation after generation of children. Every single coffee mug he had ever received as a gift sat on top of the bookcases that lined his office. He had pictures of every class he had ever taught tacked to his office wall above his desk. Students adored him. Parents revered him. Fellow teachers sang his praises. Even birds would perch outside his classroom window and sing sweetly while he taught.

Mr. Red had devoted his entire life to teaching. He lived, breathed, ate and slept teaching. His doctor warned him to slow down, to take up a hobby, to take a vacation, to rest and relax, but Mr. Red would have none of it. There was always more marking to do, always ways to improve his lesson plan, always another interesting bulletin board display waiting to be created. Perhaps it was inevitable that Mr. Red, one cloudy Thursday morning, would be forced to take a little break one way or the other.

No one knew what had happened to their teacher Mr. Red that day. Some say that he wore his beige tie once too often. Others say that he accidentally poured some sour milk into his cereal. Nobody knew for sure. What was certain was the children in his grade five class were more than a little confused when their new teacher, Mr. Green, introduced himself.

"Good morning, children. Mr. Red will be away for a few days, and I will be teaching this class in his place. My name is Mr. Green."

The children were puzzled. Their confusion resulted from the strange fact that Mr. Green looked exactly like Mr. Red. Identical. He had the same 1950s hairstyle. He wore the same tattered tweed jacket. His left ear was noticeably larger than his right one. He wore the same beige tie.

Kathleen, one of the more outspoken students in the class, finally broke the silence. "Is this an April Fool's joke, Mr. Red? I thought it had to be April."

But the new teacher snapped back, "My name is Mr. Green, and you will address me as such."

She smiled impishly. If it was a joke, Kathleen decided she would play along. "Okay, Mr. Green, whatever you say," she said. "I brought some birthday cake for Mr. Red, but since he's not here, would you like some?" She took out a small birthday cake that had been sitting inside her desk.

Mr. Green grinned approvingly, approached Kathleen's desk and then put his entire hand into her birthday cake.

"Hey, what are you doing?" cried Kathleen.

With his mouth full of cake, Mr. Green wagged his finger and said, "Never interrupt me while I'm eating someone else's cake."

Kathleen stuck out her bottom lip. "But you ruined it."

"Yes, that's life," said Mr. Green as he sucked the last bit of pink icing from his fingertips. Then he turned to the class and added, "I hope you children realize that I saved you today from a lifetime of obesity and heartache. Just look at my fingers. That cake was full of empty calories."

The students stared at each other in disbelief. How could a teacher that looked so similar to Mr. Red be so different?

"Now, it's time to continue with our favourite story, *Dr. Jekyll and Mr. Hyde*," continued Mr. Green. "You will all take turns reading as I go through your lunches to see if there's anything else that poses a dangerous caloric risk to your good health."

"But what will we eat, Mr. Green?" asked Amy, perhaps the next most precocious child in the class.

Mr. Green let out a sigh of disgust. "It's always about you, isn't it!"

"But I was just—"

"How can you even think about eating when so many children around the world are starving at this very moment?" Mr. Green took a humongous bite out of Richard's jellyroll before he added, "But since you only care about filling your hungry stomachs, we'll trade lunches and you can have mine. It will be cow tongues and lima beans for everyone."

The class moaned in unison except for Richard, who said quietly to himself, "Mmmm, cow tongues, my favourite."

The children dutifully opened their books. Most heeded what Mr. Green said and read silently as they awaited in horror for their share of Mr. Green's lunch. Edward Von Bighead, however, never did anything quietly. Mr. Red had always tolerated his tomfoolery. Mr. Green would not.

Eddie had a coughing fit that lasted quite some time. He then dropped a book on the floor accidentally. And somehow, when he went to sharpen his pencil, he opened the door to the cage of Hammy, the class's pet hamster.

"Oops," said Eddie in an overly loud voice. "I don't know how that happened."

"Edward, take your seat," said Mr. Green.

Edward was smirking when he replied. "What? I didn't do anything."

"Yes, Edward, you didn't do anything. You never have, and you never will. You see, Edward," said Mr. Green as he stood at the blackboard with a piece of chalk poised in his hand. "Here is your life," he said as he drew a big circle, "a big zero." Pleased with his insight, Mr. Green added matter-of-factly, "Class, we are now going to have a surprise quiz on World War II."

Sandra, a rather shy and sweet girl, raised her trembling hand and said, "Bb-b-ut, Mr. Green. W-w-e haven't studied World War II."

"I know. That's why it's such a surprise." And Mr. Green happily began handing out the test papers, humming softly an evil little tune.

Just as he delivered the last paper, Tara, a quick and nimble student, captured Hammy Hamster who was scurrying on the floor. "Mr. Red, I mean, Mr. Green, I caught Hammy. Should I put him in his cage?"

"Yes, put him back in the cage. It'll be easier to find him for this afternoon's science experiment."

Tara shrieked, "You're not going to dissect poor little Hammy?"

"Well, it's either Hammy or it's Edward. Would you rather we dissect Edward instead? We'll have a class vote."

The children looked into their teacher's cold, vacant eyes and decided Mr. Green wasn't very nice, not very nice at all, except for Richard, who strangely smiled and looked out the window into a future that no one else could see.

So the class proceeded. The students wrote a surprise test on a subject they knew nothing about. They ate their cow tongues and lima beans. They reluctantly dissected Hammy rather than Edward and bid Hammy a sad farewell.

"Well, children," said Mr. Green at 3:00 PM, "I think we've accomplished a lot here today. You've all taken the first steps toward learning that life is full of disappointments.

Edward's come to accept that he's going nowhere. And with a little help from Hammy, we've all learned a great deal about rodent biology." Mr. Green rubbed his hands together as his eyes gleamed with anticipation. "I can't wait to see what we'll learn tomorrow."

Upon hearing these words, a chill went through the class. Some wondered if they could inject themselves with small pox. Others contemplated enrolling themselves overnight in military school.

The next day came too quickly for the children, and to their dismay and disappointment, Mr. Green was there eager to greet them at 9:00 AM

"Hello, sir," said Kathleen meekly as she marched as quickly as possible to her desk.

"Hello," said Sandra, shaking nervously.

"Hello, students," said a cheery Mr. Green. "I hope you all had a good rest."

The students all bobbed their heads up and down in unison, fully expecting Mr. Green to do something horrible. But he didn't. Instead, Mr. Green took out some candies and offered them to the class. Next, he told them a wonderful story about some dancing penguins who managed to stop global warming. After that, he took his students on a field trip to the zoo.

"Mr. Green," said Amy with a trembling voice, "are you sure you're feeling okay?"

The man before Amy stared at her blankly. "Mr. Green? Who's he?"

Amy gulped. It appeared that Mr. Green had once again become Mr. Red. From that day forward, everything was more or less as it once was. Hammy was replaced by a hamster named Dave. The birds sang sweetly. Parents and the principal once again revered Mr. Red, and fellow teachers sang his praise.

Every now and then, however, when the students dared look out the corner of their eyes, they could see the shadow of a grinning Mr. Green inviting them to join his class.

The Beetle Matador

Though many people have heard of the jitterbug, the Charleston, the salsa and the cha-cha, few have ever heard of the rhinoceros twist. It is a dance which, oddly enough, was invented in a tiny bullring not that long ago by a twelve year old boy and a rhinoceros beetle.

Harvey Caper was an average student. He was okay at math, so-so at science and reasonably proficient in language arts. It was perhaps because he was so average in everything that he had no idea what to do with the rest of his life. And so, on the sound advice of his guidance counsellor, he decided to visit a fortune teller.

"Ah yes," said the fortune teller as she looked into her crystal ball. "I see a great future for you as a . . . " she hesitated for a moment, as she rubbed her temples, "a fighter."

Harvey's eyes widened with delight. "A fighter?" he exclaimed. He pictured himself a fighter pilot in the cockpit of an F-22 Raptor.

"Yes," said the woman, continuing to rub her temples. "I see crowds cheering, roses being thrown at your feet. You will be a great . . . beetle fighter!"

Harvey's smile began to disappear. Nothing in the world thrilled him less than the thought of being a bug exterminator. "Are you sure of your facts?" asked Harvey. "Perhaps you should consult the crystal ball one more time."

"No," said the fortune teller. "A beetle fighter. It is your destiny."

Harvey sighed. "So where must I go to be trained for this, uh, great career?"

"You must go to El Paso. A small arena awaits you," she looked down once again at the ball, "near the border, where Chihuahua Street meets Calleros Court. There you will meet a great man named Hernandez who will teach you everything you need to know."

Harvey thanked her half-heartedly and left. Normally, Harvey would not be permitted to make such a long trip away from home. But since it was his summer vacation, and since his Aunt Wanda lived just outside El Paso, Harvey was allowed to go. He only had to promise his parents that he would stay with his aunt. Unfortunately, his aunt was more than a little crazy.

I hope you like sleeping in the chicken coop," she would say each night. Harvey, having little choice, spent the entire summer sleeping with eggs falling down on his head. Though Harvey was less than impressed with his living arrangements, he soon found the beetle ring and his would-be teacher, Hernandez.

"Hello," said Harvey one hot and hazy July morning as he strolled into the beetle ring.

Hernandez looked the boy up and down. Hernandez was an older man, probably in his mid- to late fifties. His skin was leathery and he had deep crow's feet around his eyes. "So you are the young boy the fortune teller told me about," said the man. "Have you ever been in a beetle ring before?"

Harvey shook his head. "No."

"Then you are not ready," said Hernandez matter-of-factly. "To fight the beetle, you must think like the beetle." Then he got down on the ground on all fours and said, "You must *be* the beetle."

Harvey scrunched up his nose. "How will I ever learn that?"

Hernandez put his arms around the boy's shoulder. "By studying them day and night." He took a photograph out of his wallet. "Do you see this?" he asked as he pointed to a rather large beetle with a horn between its eyes. "It's a rhinoceros beetle. It is your enemy. You must learn to love it before you hate it."

Harvey looked at the beetle with disbelief in his eyes. "But it's so small."

"And that's what makes it so dangerous," said Hernandez through clenched teeth. "You see this limp?" he said as he took a few steps. "I lost my focus for one second in the ring and that rhinoceros beetle lunged at me with the precision of a surgeon. It pierced me right through the Achilles tendon." Hernandez put his hand across his heart. "If it wasn't for that rodeo clown, I would have been a dead man."

"How come those beetles are so deadly?"

"It's part of their training. Rhinoceros beetles study humans. Generation after generation. They know all about human anatomy. They know exactly where to strike to inflict the most pain."

Harvey took another look at the picture. "But they look so harmless."

"Don't be fooled by their dull eyes," warned the rhinoceros beetle matador. "It is all part of their disguise." He looked off into the distance, perhaps remembering his own past in the ring, "There is a dangerous intelligence behind that crusty shell. They may look innocent enough with their tiny legs, but they are the very definition of strength. They can lift large objects, and trust me, when they strike, they do so without mercy."

Harvey pulled away from the man's half-crazed eyes. "Then why do you do it? The fame, the money, the free egg salad sandwiches?" he asked.

The man pursed his lips. "Young boy, there are two types of men in this world: those who understand why we must face the rhinoceros beetle, and those who do not understand such things." Then he looked up at the boy and asked, "Which type of man are you?"

Harvey gazed down at his sneakers.

The man smiled. "Perhaps you will find out in the ring."

Days passed and Harvey trained hard. First, he waved his small red handkerchief in front of ladybugs. Then, he moved on to earwigs. Soon he was dueling with silverfish. By the end of the second week, he was in the ring with his first beetle, a dung beetle. It was not as ferocious as the rhinoceros beetle, but it was a beetle nonetheless.

Two more weeks passed, and the day of Harvey's first real fight with the dreaded rhinoceros beetle arrived. Peering through a crack in the ringmaster's room, he could see a giant stuffed beetle mounted on the ring master's desk. Behind the desk were framed pictures of past rhinoceros beetle fights. Not wanting to disturb the two men inside who were currently engaged in a discussion, Harvey listened to the conversation through a crack in the door.

"Oh yes, I remember Philippe," said the ringmaster. "His career was promising, but then when he was gored by that one old granddaddy beetle, he was finished."

The man at the other side of the desk asked, "How about the boy? Do you really think he has any chance of winning?"

The fat ring master laughed. "Twenty to one, against the boy."

Harvey had heard enough. He burst into the office. "I'm here for my fight," he said as bravely as a man facing his own impending doom could.

The ringmaster gave the boy a condescending smile. "What is your price?" he asked.

"Three egg salad sandwiches and some rice pudding," said Harvey.

"Your price is high," glinted the man as he looked out into the noonday sun. "Do you think I have lots of extra rice lying around? I will give you the standard two egg salad sandwiches and nothing more."

Harvey dug in his heels, "I am sorry Senior to be so stubborn, but seeing as it is likely that I will be speared to death by the beetle's mighty horn in front of your cheering customers, I do not think one extra sandwich and a little rice pudding is so much to ask for."

"I am a man willing to compromise," said the Ringmaster, "two egg salad sandwiches and half a bowl of pudding."

"Three egg salad sandwiches and a full bowl of rice pudding," the boy said flatly, "or the crowd will see nothing today and you will have to refund them all their pesos."

The fat ringmaster grinned. "You have guts. I like guts." Motioning the other man to bring the boy some food, he said, "Very well then, you'll have your three egg salad sandwiches and your bowl of rice pudding. Let's just hope you're alive at the end of the day to enjoy them."

Harvey gave the man a hard flat stare and then left. As he walked toward the ring, he was met by Hernandez.

"Here," said Hernandez as he put something into the boy's hand.

"What is it?" said Harvey.

"A good luck charm, a baby toe I lost in the ring a long time ago," said Hernandez. "It was a good toe. It served me well," he said as he put the toe necklace around Harvey's neck. "Now it will serve you."

Harvey smiled. "Thank-you, Hernandez. I will try to remember everything you've taught me."

Hernandez insisted, "There is no try, young Matador. There is do and there is not do, but in the ring, there is no try." Hernandez smiled at his student and the two parted.

One o'clock arrived and Harvey entered the ring on the back of a Galapagos turtle. Needless to say, they had started their journey to the ring rather early that morning.

"Ole," screamed the fans.

Harvey waved his matador cap and took out his blood-red, ten-inch handkerchief. Bending down low, he scanned the arena for his enemy. And then, he saw him come out from a crack in the wall, a six inch nasty beast with nasty beetle eyes and nasty beetle skin. Never before had he seen anything uglier. Mysteriously enough, the beetle had at that moment exactly the same thought.

There was another round of applause from the arena and then the arena door closed. It was then that Harvey knew things were getting serious. Harvey shook the handkerchief slightly. The rhinoceros beetle charged at the piece of cloth, his head down, but then changed direction at the last second and gored the rodeo clown that was standing close by.

"Boo," shouted the crowds.

Disappointed that the beetle had not been drawn to him, Harvey shook the handkerchief more violently to attract the beetle's attention. His stare was hard and unflinching. So was the beetle's. He put the handkerchief in front of his body. This time, he would bring the beetle in much closer.

The beetle's eyes followed the alluring piece of fabric. He charged but Harvey moved his body out of the way at the last second.

"Ole!" yelled the crowd.

Filled with pride, Harvey turned and took a bow. This was his near fatal mistake, for as he did so, the beetle ran up behind him and pierced his ankle. It was now the beetle's turn to take a bow.

Humiliated by the beetle's sneak attack, Harvey grabbed on to one of the beetle's back legs. As he did so, the rhinoceros beetle broke into a slow gallop and pulled him around the ring. Harvey let go of the leg and pulled out his sword. As he did so, the rhinoceros beetle faced him and stuck out its horn. The crowd went silent.

For the next seventeen minutes, all that could be heard in the beetle ring was the clanging of horn against mettle as the two enemies fought. Then, when both horn and sword were worn down to a nub, the two began to circle each other like crabs in a ring.

"So it comes down to this," said Harvey, "hand to beetle leg combat."

The beetle snickered as only a beetle can. At first the two just tiptoed, pranced and minced around the ring.

Then the rhinoceros beetle lunged at Harvey's feet and the two of them started to wrestle.

Now it is a known fact in the matador world that a rhinoceros beetle can lift more than eight hundred and fifty times its weight over its head. So naturally, the beetle put the matador over his head and spun him around without even breaking a sweat.

When the crowd saw this, they cheered. Some of the smaller spectators even started to prance and mince and spin the larger spectators over their heads.

"Why, it's a new dance," shouted one of the teenagers.

"Yes, the rhinoceros twist," shouted another.

Hearing the reaction of the crowd, Harvey and the rhinoceros beetle stopped fighting. They stopped hating. They looked up at the spotlight and the cheering crowds and decided that rather than fight to their death, they would dance as though their very lives depended upon it.

The crowd marvelled as the rhinoceros beetle and Harvey did the jitterbug and the Charleston. They joined in when they did the conga and the hustle. And at the end of the evening, everyone was so thrilled that they decided to turn the beetle ring into a dance club, the only one in the world where you will ever see the rhinoceros twist.

Flowers for Theodore

Babies are babies. At least that's what Mr. and Mrs. Gordon thought before Theodore was born. The Gordons had always wanted a smart baby. They wanted, in fact, the smartest baby in the world.

Before Theodore was born, Mr. and Mrs. Gordon did everything they could to encourage their son's development, and their efforts went well beyond merely playing Mozart and Beethoven loud enough for their unborn son to hear—that was just the beginning. Mr. and Mrs. Gordon agreed there was no time like the present to begin their son's education in earnest, and they took turns talking to him about a variety of subjects. Mr. Gordon stuck mainly to the maths and sciences. Mrs. Gordon talked at length about history, literature and philosophy. At breakfast they would debate ethics or talk about the finer points of quantum physics. At lunch they would review some calculus or discuss the fall of the Roman Empire. Dinner would end with some dramatic poetry readings or perhaps Mr. Gordon's explanation of the periodic table. Of course, at all times, a Mozart CD or a Beethoven CD could be heard playing in the background.

Soon the happy day arrived and their baby was born. Now, as Mr. Gordon had been warned, all babies at first look a little like lizards, but Theodore had a total absence of any quality resembling cuteness. Rather, when Mrs. Gordon asked how their baby looked, Mr. Gordon told her the baby looked tired and wrinkled like an old man. More upsetting to both of them, their son surprisingly spoke like an old man. Just a few moments after his arrival, their newborn baby spoke in full sentences without stumbling on a single syllable. The first words out of his mouth were, "What's up, doc?" The doctor was understandably flummoxed. One might imagine that Mr. and Mrs. Gordon were equally perplexed, but as they looked down at their shockingly intelligent son babbling away in complete sentences, they knew that they themselves were the cause behind his genius. At first they were excited, but there was also some worry just underneath the surface of their happiness.

"Look how old Theodore looks!" exclaimed Mrs. Gordon.

Mr. Gordon tried his best to reassure his wife. "All babies look old, honey. Perhaps ours looks a little older than most, but by and large, that's the way they come." Mrs. Gordon, however, was not persuaded.

There were a few other things that were unusual about Theodore. Just a few days after coming home, when it was time to feed Theodore, he insisted on drinking his formula on the rocks out of a real glass and not from a baby bottle. Then the Gordons heard him remark wistfully, "I'm old, I'm old, I will wear my trousers rolled."

Mr. and Mrs. Gordon looked at the baby in astonishment.

"Our baby is . . ." Mr. Gordon stopped mid-sentence.

"I know," said Mrs. Gordon completing his sentence. "An old man."

"Whatever shall we do?" said Mr. Gordon.

Mrs. Gordon stared hard at the crib. "I guess we should take him to see a child psychologist. Maybe she can talk him out of it."

The next afternoon they took their son to see child psychologist Dr. Helga Frauleinikoffski, who quickly ascertained that quoting poetry was not the only odd ability their son had been born with. Dr. Helga, as she had her patients call her, took the entire afternoon to study Theodore.

She observed that he walked, for one thing, without stumbling or teetering in the least. This just looked a little strange, as he was rather a smallish baby to begin with, and one did not generally see newborn infants walking upright under their own power. He could read, which was also very strange, but stranger still was his instant disagreement with practically every editorial column he read and his total aversion to the comic section. Perhaps most disturbing was young Theodore's penchant for disagreeing with every parenting decision Mr. or Mrs. Gordon made and his intense desire to debate their decisions at length. Theodore explained to Dr. Helga that his parents meant well but had collected a hodgepodge of popular parenting wisdom that often contradicted itself.

It was Theodore who told Dr. Helga about the constant lectures and classical music he had to endure before his birth. Dr. Helga realized that Mr. and Mrs. Gordon may have gotten a little more than they had wished for. They both had an inkling that they might have overdone it on their early education program, but Dr. Helga confirmed this with her diagnosis.

Never enjoying delivering bad news, Dr. Helga tried to use her most compassionate voice when she conveyed her findings. "Yes, all the knowledge you've fed your baby before his birth has certainly had its effect; unfortunately, it appears to have been a little too effective, by the looks of it."

"Is there nothing we can do?" asked Mrs. Gordon.

"No, nothing," Dr. Helga replied. "Your child simply knows too much for his own good, and the weight of this knowledge has made him old before his time. It's very rare to see it happen to this degree, but actually, it occurs far more often than most people realize."

"What should we do?" asked Mr. Gordon.

"Treat him more immaturely," Dr. Helga replied. "Try not to let it bother you. If we are lucky, in time, the natural equilibrium will slowly return between age and behaviour."

"But how long?" asked an anxious Mrs. Gordon.

"These things have a habit of working themselves out over a few years," Dr. Helga answered. "It may, though, take a few decades, but in the end you will discover that the two of you can and will experience all the joys you dreamed of. Now off you go, and stop all your worrying."

For a few days, the Gordons were rather successful at overlooking just how unusual their baby acted and how old he appeared, but their ability to pretend everything was normal soon evaporated.

The next day, the Gordons took Theodore to the office of a different child psychologist, Dr. Ida Psyche, in the hopes of getting a second opinion and some different answers.

"And so, little Theodore," asked Dr. Psyche, "what is it that makes you think you are so old?"

Theodore gave the doctor a grimace. "I don't think I'm old, doctor. I am old."

The doctor nodded her head. "Hmmm, I see, but Theodore you were only born a few days ago."

"Yes," said the baby sadly, "I felt even older then."

The doctor scratched her chin. Noticing Theodore fingering some mutual fund charts beside her coffee table, she snatched them out of his hand. "Perhaps if you spent less time looking through the financial pages and more time with stuffed animals you wouldn't feel so mature."

"But retirement, worrying about my future grandchildren's future, talking about the way things used to be, that's my life," Theodore lamented.

The three adults stared at each other. At last, Dr. Psyche spoke. "Well," she said, gathering up her things, "there's nothing I can do at this point. Hopefully, when he hits kindergarten, he'll grow out of it."

Listening to her advice and hoping it would help, the Gordons enrolled Theodore in kindergarten three days later. After spending only two days there, however, they got a distressing call from Theodore's kindergarten teacher.

"I'm sorry," said the teacher, "but your son is just too advanced for this class. I think he would be much happier if you put him straight into high school."

Mr. and Mrs. Gordon hugged each other. "He's just growing up so fast," said Mrs. Gordon tearfully.

"I know," said Mr. Gordon. "I guess we'll have to enjoy what's left of his youth while we still can."

So the Gordons sent Theodore to high school. Like his kindergarten teacher, his high school teacher also felt that Theodore was too old for his classroom. He recommended that Theodore enrol in a graduate classroom at a nearby university. After Theodore had spent less than a week at university, his professor decided that Theodore was more qualified to teach the class than she was, and she left her classroom for a year-long emergency sabbatical. From that point on, Theodore's rise in academia was meteoric, to say the least.

Receiving a Nobel Prize by the time he was two, a dinner was held in Theodore's honour. Theodore was seated in a large high chair in the centre of the room, while his parents fed him on either side.

"So what is the secret to having a Nobel Prize–winning son?" asked a writer from *Literary Digest.*

Mrs. Gordon scooped some stewed carrots off her dress. "Well," she said thoughtfully, "no secret really. I guess we've just been blessed with a son that is more mature and more intelligent than any of us." Mrs. Gordon and Mr. Gordon had decided sometime just after Theodore's first birthday to avoid discussing the roots of their son's genius with reporters. They told each other it was to protect their son from too many people prying, but both Mrs. and Mr. Gordon knew, rather, it was simply to avoid confronting their own guilt from pushing their son too far too fast.

For the next few years, Theodore continued to work at the university and write his ground-breaking manuscript on the secret Pig Latin society of Outer Mongolia. And then, one sunny Thursday, something happened that put his research on hold.

"Mother," said Theodore, "I can't seem to finish writing this manuscript. It's as though," he hesitated for a moment, "all I can think about is football."

Mrs. Gordon looked quizzically at her child. Never before had he mentioned such an ordinary, frivolous idea. Inspecting him more closely, she noticed something unusual about his skin. Instead of being dried and prunelike, it was slightly moist and stretchy, as though he were a man just shy of middle age. Mrs. Gordon said nothing for a few moments, trying to collect her thoughts. Then, looking deeply into her son's slightly wrinkled face, she suggested, "Why don't you go outside and play?"

Theodore's brows knitted together. "But I have so many important things to do."

Mrs. Gordon put a hand under her son's chin. "They can wait," she assured him.

And so Theodore, for the first time in his life, played football. Though he dropped the ball every time, he enjoyed it nonetheless. Subsequently, he started playing several other games, including European fish slapping with his Scandinavian neighbours and full contact "Mother, May I?" with the two teens across the street.

Two weeks later, Mr. Gordon received a call from the university. "Your son has missed teaching five classes this month," said a gruff voice. "Therefore, we'll have to fire him."

Mr. and Mrs. Gordon discussed the situation with Theodore, who was busy playing basketball in his driveway.

"That's cool," said Theodore as he attempted to slam-dunk the ball into the hoop. "And by the way, the name's not Theodore. It's Teddy."

"Teddy?" his parents asked together.

"Yeah," Theodore smirked, "that's what all the girls call me."

Mr. and Mrs. Gordon looked at one another. "Oh no," cried Mrs. Gordon, "our boy is growing down."

Mr. Gordon tried to comfort his wife, "Well, honey, look at it this way: at least we'll never have to worry about our boy growing up and disappointing us again."

Mrs. Gordon nodded. "I guess we'd better start stocking the fridge with pizzas."

The Gordons returned to Dr. Frauleinikoffski to find out what was happening to their son and to get her advice on what they should do next.

She spent time with Theodore and was genuinely pleased to present her findings to the Gordons. "Your son is finding the equilibrium that has been missing for all these years," she began.

"But how, and why now?" asked Mr. Gordon.

"The cataclysmic shock your son's neural network initially sustained in infancy slowly has subsided, like the melting of an enormous emotional glacier. The deep subconscious connections have realigned, and this has cascaded across the entire emotive spectrum, manifesting itself in behaviours much more akin to a younger and more immature personality." The Gordons pretended to understand what she was talking about, but in truth, it sounded like a mouthful of gobbledygook. More encouraging, though, Theodore didn't understand a single word either. He just wanted to know if he could stop wasting all his time and get back to some quality recreational activities.

And so Theodore, or "Teddy," as he now called himself, began to throw parties—wild ones, with marathon games of Twister and pin the tail on the donkey. This went on for several more weeks until Teddy was demoted back to elementary school.

"Ah man, do I have to do my homework?" complained Teddy to his parents.

"Yes, you do," said his mother. "If you don't, how else are you going to grow up and . . ." She stopped herself.

"Yes?" said Teddy brightly.

"Get a part-time job," she finished.

"Oh yeah," smiled Teddy. "Good thinking, Mom, I really can use some extra coin."

The years went by, and as Teddy's parents slowly grew older, Teddy was getting younger every day at an accelerated pace. Though he was technically in his late-thirties, he had the face and mind of a six-year-old.

"Can I have some ice cream, Mom?" he would beg at dinner. "I want some ice cream!"

"No, Teddy. Junk food is not good for growing boys." His father paused for a second and added, "It's not good for adults either."

"No fair," said Teddy disappointedly. "Can I go upstairs and play with my cars and my mini-stick?"

"Alright," said his mother, "but no slapshotting the cars into the wall; you'll leave marks."

"Yes, Mom," said Teddy as he ran off to find his tiny replica hockey stick and his favourite toy cars. Dashing up the stairs, Teddy stumbled on the dissertation he had written for his post-doctoral thesis when he had been a one year old.

"Hey, look at this book," he said as he picked it up and sat it on his head. "Sure is heavy. I wonder who wrote it?"

"You did," sighed his father, "but you're too young to remember writing it."

"Oh," said Teddy, sticking out his bottom lip. "It looks kind of boring," Then he pointed it toward the chimney and said, "I wonder if we could use it for firewood."

Mr. and Mrs. Gordon looked at one another. Certainly, their dreams of their son growing up and becoming successful had come and gone all too soon. But somehow, when they saw the bright glow in Teddy's eyes, all of that didn't matter. They decided to enjoy him, just as he was. The joy of childhood had arrived almost a little too late, but they were going to enjoy every single moment they had. And so, on one bitterly cold wintry night, they burned his Nobel Prize–winning thesis and watched the glorious flickering flames with their son in quiet happiness.

Marvin the Evil Parrot

Many centuries ago, a parrot was born, an abnormal parrot. Normal perhaps on the outside, feathers and beak and such, but on the inside, this parrot was pure evil. Not only was it evil, but each of its children and its children's children was evil. In fact, the whole line right down through human history was rotten to the core and was personally responsible for every major evil event in recorded human history.

Historians would laugh at such a ridiculous statement and say that this war or that famine was due to some political, scientific or economic cause. An evil parrot could be right under their noses and they would continue to neglect any evidence that most human suffering was indeed caused by a long line of evil parrots.

The present-day heir to this lineage of evil parrotness, Marvin the Merciless, sat patiently in his cage in the window of Mel's Pet Shop waiting to fulfill his evil destiny. He sat there proudly remembering some of the evil accomplishments his ancestor parrots had performed before him.

In the fifth century, it was Marvin's ancient ancestor, the prized bird of Walter the Barbarian, whose advice led to the Barbarian's invasion of pretty much every land they could get to by horseback. In the 14th century, there was an outbreak of the black plague in nearly every hospital. Most historians still blame the unfortunate rat and perhaps the low price of pepper for spreading the plague when, in fact, it was an evil parrot. It was Marvin's great, great, great, great, great, great-grandfather who, if truth be told, was responsible for some of the worst haircuts in history and at least two potato famines.

In the 20th century, various members of Marvin's ancestry were known to have spoken with a number of cruel leaders, including Edward the Fat, Edward the Not-So-Fat and Edward the Downright Skinny. Evil is as evil does, and the 21st century was in for its own fair share of evil, as Marvin had clearly inherited the evil parrot gene from his evil father, William the Not-So-Nice.

On the second of July, Marvin the Merciless left Mel's Pet Store and became the birthday gift of one Robbie Nathaniel Schubert.

"Thank you, Mom and Dad," Robbie said, hugging his parents. He acted pleased, but secretly he had been longing for a toy race car or at least a year's subscription to *National Geographic*.

Everyone at the table ooed and awed at the splendidly coloured bird, everyone, that is, except for Grandma Wilcox.

"That parrot is evil, I tell ya," said Grandma Wilcox, "Evil!" Grandma Wilcox was a fairly crabby person with eyes that would wander off in two different directions when she spoke, making it very difficult to look her in the eye.

"Oh, Granny," Mr. Schubert laughed, "you're always complaining about something." It was true. Grandma did complain a lot.

Ignoring her son's comments, Grandma Wilcox leaned over the table and whispered into Robbie's ear, "Mark my words, boy, that bird is trouble. Kill it before it's too late."

Robbie attempted to push his chair away from his grandmother. "Sure, Granny, maybe after dinner." Then he turned to his parents. "Can I be excused now? I want to play with my parrot."

"Of course, Robbie," his mother said with a smile, and Robbie ran upstairs so quickly that no one heard him muttering his disappointment to Marvin the Merciless about getting only a dumb bird for a gift and not getting a fascinating toy race car with duel turbo engines.

Now Robbie was a good boy. He always did his homework, he never went to school unwashed and he was never late. The worst thing Robbie had ever done up until that point in his life was perhaps capture a cricket and keep it as a desk pet for three days before freeing it in the middle of the playground. But after having received Marvin the Merciless, things began to change. Following Marvin's instructions, Robbie placed coloured mothballs in his father's healthy Fruit-A-Bix cereal box.

In his mother's underwear drawer, he liberally sprinkled itching powder and in the dog's dish, he placed a heaping mound of cat food.

These evil deeds also showed up in his behaviour at school. Robbie put sugar in the saltshakers in the cafeteria and hid mustard in one of his classmates' gym shoes. Then he placed a couple of snakes in his teacher's desk, and he deliberately forgot to return his library books on time. Marvin would praise Robbie for his evil behaviour while Robbie slept, and he would plant the seeds for further evil shenanigans.

Robbie's appearance began to change as well. Instead of dressing in his school uniform, he went to class in a black suit not wearing any shoes. His hair, which was usually neatly combed, was now wild and crazy with evilness. Instead of carrying a copy of *National Geographic* in his knapsack, he now carried Sun Tzu's *The Art of War*.

"What's the matter with you?" said Mrs. Schubert as she came down to breakfast one morning.

"Nothing," said Robbie as he needled a voodoo doll of his teacher. "Nothing at all."

Mr. Schubert looked at his worried wife and reassured her. "Maybe it's just a stage he's going through."

Unknown to his parents at the time, that stage would last for many years. What had started off innocently enough in public school went on into high school and then university. By the time Robbie was in his fourth year science class, he had learned how to make many explosive devices and was working on a chemical compound that would make ground beef stick to frying pans and angel food cakes fall.

"Very good," said the parrot to Robbie as he slept one night. "Because of your evil in the world, more people will be overcome with depression in their kitchens."

"I am glad you are pleased that I have dedicated my life to evil as you instructed," said Robbie in a sleepy, robotic voice.

"Yes, I am very pleased," Marvin said. "But now you must take over the world."

Robbie replied in his sleep, "Take over the world?"

"Yes," said the parrot. "Sooner or later, every great evil leader has to try to take over the world. It's standard evildoer practice. I will summon my evil powers to help you."

"Thank you, master," said Robbie mechanically as he rolled over and hugged his teddy bear. Marvin talked at great length for the rest of the night, planting the greatest of his evil ideas in Robbie's absorbent mind.

Robbie awoke the next day eager to begin Marvin's plan for world domination. Everything made perfect sense. The part about taking over control of the world's supply of sesame seed bagels and low-fat cream cheese made sense. The part about destroying every microwave oven in the world so that parents could no longer cook for their children made sense. Even the part about the armless leprechauns and the no-neck giraffes kind of made sense. Of course, the first part of the plan involved taking over the local television station and broadcasting an evil message to gather an evil army of followers. Pleased by Robbie's enthusiasm, Marvin rolled his eyes back into his head, puffed his feathers in a particularly evil fashion and said, "Let us begin."

Marvin truly believed that he had thought of everything; however, Marvin had not thought of everything. He hadn't considered the part a very old and very crabby grandmother might play in ruining his evil plan. As Marvin and Robbie came downstairs and walked into the kitchen, Marvin was quite surprised by Grandma Wilcox's ambush.

"I knew it!" she cried. "I knew you were up to no good."

Marvin did not respond, but Robbie said, "Grandma, we're just going for a walk. Marvin wouldn't hurt a caterpillar."

"Your parents said I was crazy, but I know evil when I see evil, and I'm gonna stop it, right here, right now!"

"Quick, Robbie, run!" Marvin motioned Robbie to head for the door, but Robbie could only stand there and watch with frozen curiosity.

"Okay, parrot," said Grandma Wilcox as she grabbed two salad tongs out of her pockets, "it's show time."

"So be it," said Marvin, laughing his most evil laugh.

"I remember what you did to that nice man down the street," said Grandma Wilcox as she slowly began to approach the parrot like an aging gunfighter. "He never was the same after spending that afternoon with you."

"He was weak," squawked Marvin. Then he pointed his claw in Grandma Wilcox's direction and said seductively, "Come over to the dark side, honey."

"Never," she hissed. Grandma Wilcox made a mad grab for Marvin but missed, and Marvin, in return, splattered a large parrot dropping on her head. "I'll get you for that," Grandma Wilcox snarled.

"One for Marvin the Merciless. Zero for Granny." Then Marvin smirked and said, "Hey, I can't help if you're old and slow."

Grandma Wilcox knew that Marvin the Merciless was right. She was slower than he, but she was also more patient. She knew that if she just sat back and let Marvin come to her, sooner or later, he would let down his guard.

"So, Marvin," said Grandma Wilcox with fake interest, "tell me the secret of your evil power."

Never shy of boasting about his ancestors, Marvin began, "Well, it all dates back to before the fifth century . . . " And for several minutes, Marvin told the story of his entire lineage and was so caught up in the telling of it that he did not notice Grandma Wilcox's salad tongs ever so slowly inching closer and closer toward his feathery neck.

"Gotcha!" cried Grandma Wilcox, her salad tongs around Marvin's throat.

"What are you going to do to me?" squawked Marvin fearfully. He struggled, but there was no escaping her salad tong grip.

"Something somebody should have done a long time ago," said Grandma Wilcox. Then she hobbled over to the kitchen sink and poured some water into a pot.

"You're going to eat me," whimpered Marvin.

"No, I'm gonna clean your soul" said Grandma Wilcox as she added some soap to the pot and put Marvin in it.

"This is horrible!" cried Marvin. "I feel so, so . . . " Marvin felt the hot soapy water begin to warm his cold bird flesh, "so happy."

"It's nice, isn't it," said Grandma Wilcox. "Now call off your plan to destroy the world."

"No!" said Marvin defiantly.

"Alright then," said Grandma Wilcox. "I'm going to clean you in hotter water."

"It won't make any difference," chirped Marvin. "I'll just become evil again. It's in my genes."

"Maybe so," said Grandma Wilcox. "But I think as long as someone washes your soul regularly, you'll never harm anyone else." She filled the basin with hotter water and continued scrubbing and cleaning the captured bird. And Grandma Wilcox might have been right about cleaning Marvin's soul and she might have been right about him turning good, but nobody will ever know for sure. At least Grandma Wilcox was right about Marvin never hurting anyone again, since it would be very difficult for Marvin to do any evil at all after being accidentally cooked.

"What should we do now, Granny?" said Robbie.

"Well, Robbie," his grandmother said as she turned away from her pot of accidental parrot soup, "how about you and I go to the pet store, and Granny will buy you a nice little puppy."

No Exit

It was a Tuesday night like most any other Tuesday night. Men and women were stuck in traffic coming home from work. Students were busy talking to their friends on their cell phones. Sixteen-year-old Katelin Lemon had gone grocery shopping for her mom.

Katelin began to put her groceries on the checkout counter. There was a bunch of bananas, a pear, a green apple, some blueberries, and a cherry pie. She had forgotten something, but she wasn't sure what it was.

"Will that be all, miss?" asked the cashier.

Katelin looked at the fifteen-year-old boy behind the counter. He seemed familiar, almost too familiar, like the kind of person that people see in their school yearbooks but never quite remember their name. She asked slowly, "Do I know you?"

The boy shook his head. "I don't think so," he said as he rang in her produce.

"But I'm sure I've seen you before," Katelin persisted. She looked at the boy's face more closely. "Perhaps you went to school with my younger sister, Lesliola Lemon?"

The checkout boy shifted his eyes uncomfortably. "Look, miss, I don't know you. I've never even seen you before."

"Are you sure? Those beady eyes, those cheekbones: they look so familiar," Katelin said.

"Ya, I'm sure." His voice trailed off as he put the last of her groceries into a bag.

Embarrassed, Katelin quickly grabbed her groceries and made her way toward the exit. Oddly enough, she did not remember paying for her groceries. Odder still, she could not remember where the exit was located.

"I don't understand," she muttered to herself as she continued to walk around the perimeter of the store. There were windows and signs but no exits to be seen. And when she tried to listen for the sound of an electronic door, all she could hear was a faint buzzing noise.

After several more minutes of walking aimlessly, Katelin was approached by a kind old man pushing his shopping cart. He was a rather odd-looking man with enormous eyes, but his voice was full of compassion. "Can I help you?" he said. "You seem a little lost."

"Yes," said a frustrated Katelin. "I know this might sound crazy, but I can't seem to find a way out of this store."

"Oh," said the man thoughtfully. "The exit is right over . . . hmmm . . . that's odd. I thought it was right over there." The old man went strangely silent, as though he himself had become completely befuddled by the disappearing exit. And then, with an arched eyebrow, he asked, "Well then, how did you and I get in here? We certainly couldn't have been born in here. We must have come in from somewhere."

Katelin put a finger to her chin. She had been in this particular store hundreds of times before, maybe even thousands of times, yet she could not seem to remember how she got in. Indeed, she could not actually remember ever entering the store. "I don't know," said Katelin.

"I see," said the old man who, for no particular reason, pulled out a lemon wedge and began sucking on its insides. "Would you like some?" he offered.

"Oh, no thank you," said Katelin, remembering her mother's advice never to take lemons from strangers.

"Okay, let's see if we can apply some logic here," said the old man. "If you don't know where the exit is, perhaps we should start by asking you something you do know."

"Sounds sensible enough to me," said Katelin.

"Good," said the old man as he began to hop around and turn, taking rapid, jerky little steps. "Now, first of all, what is your name?" he asked.

"My name is Katelin Lemon."

"Are you sure?" the old man asked, jumping around more frantically. "Are you sure you are not someone else?"

"Yes, I am sure," said Katelin as she reached for her purse to get some piece of identification, a birth certificate or driver's license, but her purse was nowhere in sight. When she turned back to speak to the old man, he too had vanished. Was it possible that he had run off with her purse? Katelin could not believe the old man would do such a thing. But where was her purse? Where was the old man? Katelin sat down right there in the middle of the aisle and had a little cry.

Before too long a kindly old woman came by humming a little tune. When she saw Katelin, she stopped and offered her some help. "What seems to be the problem, missy?"

"I can't find my way out of this store," Katelin said.

"Well, that is certainly a doozy of a problem. My name's Ardra Susan. What's yours?"

"Katelin."

"Well, Katelin, if we are going to solve your problem, we'd better start with a plan," said Ardra Susan.

"You know where the exit is then?" asked Katelin.

"No, sorry, deary, never had need for one, but we can look anyways." The old woman smiled and took Katelin by the hand. "Perhaps we could start by searching the fruit section."

Katelin nodded and the two of them made their way toward the fruit aisle, which was just past the unhealthy candy department.

"Well," said Ardra Susan, lifting up various types of brightly coloured produce, "do you see anything?"

"Nope."

"A rabbit hole, perhaps a trap door?"

"Nothing," said Katelin dejectedly.

"Then we'll just have to try the meat section," said Ardra Susan, and the two of them headed to the other side of the store. But by the time they got there, all the meat had turned back into a wobbly pyramid of apples, peaches, pears and plums.

"That's odd," said Katelin. "I thought we just did the fruit aisle."

"Yes, that sort of thing often happens around here," said Ardra Susan, and then she began walking up the side of the wall.

"That's amazing. How do you do that?" asked Katelin.

Ardra Susan smiled. "Well, you just think that the walls are made out of fly paper, and it's no problem."

Katelin looked down at her tiny feet and then began to climb up the wall, "You mean like this?"

"Yes, exactly," said Ardra Susan. And the two climbed up and up until at last they were sitting on the ceiling. Katelin was so delighted that she began to forget all about leaving the store.

"What an excellent view," said Katelin. "It's almost as though I were meant to live up here."

"Yes, yes," said Ardra Susan. "Listen, there is something I ought to tell you. Promise you won't be too mad?"

"What?" said Katelin.

"You see, for all the rumours of there being an exit, a way out of the store, there actually isn't one."

"There isn't?" Katelin asked, but she knew in her heart that Ardra Susan had told her the truth. Katelin felt the store lights dimming and Adra Susan's voice becoming dull and distant. "Ardra Susan, I can hardly hear you," said Katelin. She sensed danger in the air. With a mere tenth of a second to spare, Katelin desperately jumped out of the way of a ten-foot flyswatter crashing down around her. Katelin cried out for help, darted this way and that, felt something hit her head and saw everything around her fade to black as she fell to the ground.

"Katelin, wake up, wake up," said a gentle elderly voice.

Katelin opened her eyes, only to find three fruit flies buzzing around her.

"I'm so glad she's pulled through," said a soothing voice.

"What am I doing here?" said Katelin faintly.

A fruit fly with exceptionally big eyes (even for a fruit fly) sat down beside her and said, "Yesterday you had an accident. One of the stock boys nearly finished you off with his death smacker; you've been unconscious ever since."

Katelin looked down at her body. "I'm a fruit fly?"

The youngest fruit fly laughed. "Of course you're a fruit fly. What did you think you are? A human?"

Katelin looked at the fruit that surrounded her. "But I was a human. I talked to people in the store," she protested. "I bought groceries . . . I looked for an exit."

The fruit fly with the average build petted her feeler. "Of course you did. Now try to relax."

Katelin turned her head to the floor and pounded on it with her tiny leg. "No, you don't understand. You were there, and you were there, and you were the check out boy. I want out of this box. I don't want to be a fruit fly!" she cried. "Where is the exit?"

"Sorry, deary, there is no exit," said one fruit fly as calmly as she could.

"Worse case of people-wannabe-itis I've ever seen ," said the oldest fruit fly. The other two fruit flies sighed and shook their heads.

"Will she ever recover?" asked the youngest fruit fly.

"Who can say," said the fruit fly with aging, buggy eyes. After taking a teeny-weeny bite of some lemon rind, he flew up to one of the lights and sat on the ceiling. The stock girls and boys were once again rearranging the fruit in the fruit section. It was going to be a very long day.

Little Miss Bitey

Even as a baby, it was clear that Little Miss Bitey was different. Now, not many people could remember back that far, and even those who could, could no longer remember her real name—perhaps Darla, or Carla, or Barbara. Whatever it had been originally, it was now lost forever. Not even her parents were certain what they had once named their daughter, and no birth certificate could be found anywhere to help answer the riddle. She was simply known to everyone as Little Miss Bitey. Of course, it was because of her teeth. She was, to say the least, a little bit bitey.

By about the time she was seven, hopes to correct the uniqueness of her dental structure were abandoned by her parents and the countless orthodontists they took their special child to see. "I'm sorry; there's nothing that can be done," became almost a personal mantra for Little Miss Bitey. This is not to say that she had accepted her peculiar plight with ease.

Being the only child in her school, her village and her country with teeth that looked more like wolf fangs than human teeth was not without unfortunate social consequences. Certainly her parents loved her, but there was always an underlying sense that they were a little disappointed that their daughter did not fit into normal society. The school children were at times cruel and vicious. Their taunts of "Here, wolfy" and "Here, nibbler" did nothing to enhance her self-esteem at that most critical time in her youth.

Little Miss Bitey more than a few times stared at the mirror in the quietness of her bedroom and asked, "Why me?" The reflection in the mirror held no answer; as far as she could tell, she was a hideous beast who deserved no love, no praise, no future. What she could not see, since there was no way around seeing herself except through the eyes of her fellow school children, was that the reflection in the mirror as she transformed from a child into a teen into a woman only got more beautiful each day. Little Miss Bitey could have won a thousand beauty contests if not for her pointed and dangerous teeth that terrified the narrow-minded judges who were stuck in their sad, un-pointy view of the world.

Not surprisingly, as a means to endure and at times resist the harsh society surrounding her, Little Miss Bitey began to lash out at the world. The school children would suffer the most. Their hands, arms, occasionally neck and face, were covered in bite marks. Her teachers took their share of bites. The principal was not out of harm's way, either. There was no detention, suspension, counselling session or punishment that could or would deter Little Miss Bitey from nibbling and gnashing. She bit joggers, rollerbladers and a whole variety of mail carriers. Even her parents occasionally found themselves at the wrong end of her pointed teeth. The only living creature in her line of sight that was never bitten was her cat Fluffball. One might assume that there was no reason to bite Fluffball as her teeth were even pointier than Little Miss Bitey's.

Fortunately for the world, Little Miss Bitey found a job that required little contact with people and one that gave her plenty of opportunity to use her teeth. She was a processed food inspector for a large multi-national corporation. Her job was to test the consistency of every food item they produced and provide feedback before the products were unleashed upon the world. She had a few friends, but even they would go out in public only if she promised to wear her restraining muzzle.

She would have endured her life in quiet resignation and never experienced true happiness or the deep satisfaction of being understood and celebrated by another if she had not gone to a fateful dance one Hallowe'en.

In the heart of the big city, Little Miss Bitey and her friends went to an outrageous costume party. People were not dressed as Raggedy Ann or Little Bo Peep. Rather, they were mostly dressed as werewolves, vampires and monsters of every sort. She had gone as Hannibella Lecter, with her teeth locked safely behind a caged mask. It was the only outfit her friends could agree upon that would protect them while still allowing Little Miss Bitey to join them for the evening. The night was full of music and all the monsters danced wildly.

As the music got louder, Little Miss Bitey was separated from her group of friends. It was then that she backed into him. She was apologetic and smiled an apologetic smile. His eyes were drawn to her smile and more to the point, to her pointed teeth, like a moth drawn to an electric bug zapper. "You don't need to apologize," the tall, mesmerized man said. He was dressed as a vampire: cape, teeth, fancy clothes. Soon they were off the dance floor talking a mile a minute. All the while his gaze kept returning to her sharp and dangerous teeth. In next to no time, the tall man began to tell Little Miss Bitey his story.

His name was Felix, and there was no other way to describe himself to her but to tell her that he was, in fact, a reverse vampire.

Felix had been raised by vampires, was, in fact, supposed to be a vampire, but something had gone wrong. It might have been genetic; it might have been environmental. At any rate, the very thought of biting someone or something disgusted him. He had gotten everything backwards. He could only live and survive not by biting someone, but by being bitten himself. Et voilà, a reverse vampire.

"Ridiculous," "absurd" and "silly" were all words that Little Miss Bitey replied with, but she was intrigued by his story. And the reverse vampire continued.

As a child, Felix tried biting himself but to no avail. It had to be someone or something else. He bought a Venus flytrap and put it beside his bed so that he could dangle his fingers over the side and be gently nipped during his sleep. This would give him enough energy to face another day.

When he was older, he bought some tiny piranha fish that he would take with him into the bath. They seemed to do the trick for a while, but, inevitably, he moved from tiny fish teeth to canine incisors. He bought a Doberman pinscher, a Rottweiler and an angry pit bull, but their biting was always all too infrequent for his liking.

His parents were very disturbed by his behaviour and by his refusal to bite people for sustenance. Felix had become a vegetarian.

Vampire school had been especially hard on Felix, as the other vampire children were often mean, even for vampires. They would throw tiny wooden toothpicks at his heart or pick up wreaths of garlic with rubber gloves and try to toss them around his neck. Occasionally, they would even try to push him into the sunlight at dawn.

Little Miss Bitey knew how children could sometimes be cruel and she listened sympathetically to every word of Felix's life story. Then, she told her own.

"This cage thing on your face, it has a key?" Felix, the reverse vampire, asked.

"Yes," replied Little Miss Bitey.

"Could I please have it? I would like to uncage you," he said.

"Are you sure? I must warn you that—"

"More sure than I've ever been about anything in my life," Felix interrupted with enough conviction to make Little Miss Bitey's hand reach into her pocket and give him the key.

Upon being set free, she could not resist Felix's exposed neck, and she bit him.

It was love at first bite.

The Last Day

Enid burrowed upward into the light. She had been germinating in the ground for many months and today would be, as it was for all flag flies, the first and last day of her existence on Earth.

"Hey, Enid. We made it!" cried Bernie, another flag fly who had shared the same birth pod with her.

Feeling the light touch her shell for the first time, Enid shielded her eyes with her tiny feet. "It's so bright," she said as she scuttled into the shadow of a nearby tree for protection. As her eyes slowly became adjusted to the light, her tiny smile faded. For there, under the thick canopy of leaves, were the remains of a flag fly. "We're going to die at the end of today, aren't we?" she said sadly.

Bernie's happy expression also disappeared. "I suppose so."

Enid stared back at the hole from which she came. She had lain there for what seemed like years, only to find herself cold and naked in a world she did not understand. "Twenty-four hours," said Enid.

Bernie scratched his feelers. "I guess when you put it that way, coming up into the light doesn't sound like such a good idea after all."

Enid crumpled up her body into a small ball. "I'm going back into my hole," she said.

Bernie tried to prevent Enid from going back down.

"Why should I bother? We're just going to die anyway," said Enid glumly.

"Because I'd miss you." Bernie tried his best to be cute and dance a happy dance, but Enid wouldn't listen.

Just then, a wise old owl flew overhead and landed on a nearby rock. "Can I be of assistance?" he asked.

"Yes," said Bernie, not quite sure if he should be talking to strangers, "but first I have to ask you, are you going to eat us?"

The owl hooted. "No, I just had breakfast."

"Whew, that's a relief," said Bernie. "It would be pretty horrible to be eaten in the first few minutes of life."

"Yes, it would be, but you're in luck. I am seriously stuffed," said the wise old owl, who then plucked out some mouse fur from its beak with the pointy end of a stray feather.

"Maybe being eaten would be a blessing," grumbled Enid.

Bernie put two feelers over Enid's mouth. "Don't listen to her," said Bernie. "She's just depressed because we've only got one day to live."

The wise old owl listened closely, spinning its head around. "This is a common complaint of the flag fly," said the owl. "Too much to do, and too little time to do it in."

Bernie rubbed his legs together sadly. "Well, what can I do to help her?"

"Hmm," said the wise old owl as its eyes gleamed in the morning sun, "perhaps she needs to talk to a more experienced flag fly about all this."

"Of course," said Bernie. "Someone with more knowledge." The wise old owl flew off, and Bernie thought about how he could help Enid.

Heeding the owl's advice, Bernie consulted with several other flag flies nearby and found out there was a wonderful flag fly therapy session taking place just a few trees away. Enid was not thrilled about going, but she promised Bernie that she would give it a try.

When Enid entered the therapy session, she saw many of the flag flies sitting on giant leaves, some flat and some nicely covered with pompom puffs.

"So my wife, see, she left me for this other flag fly. You know, a guy with much flashier wings and bigger eyes."

The counsellor looked suspiciously at the flag fly speaking. "And what was your role in all of this? Did you bring down some tree sap smoothies for her to drink? Did you bring her any flower petals?"

The male flag fly shook his head.

The counsellor then continued. "You see, everyone, if we want to have good things happen to us, we must take control of situations. We have to make them happen. Now," the counsellor looked at Enid, "what's your problem?"

Enid looked at her many tiny feet. "I just don't see the point of it all. I mean, you're born, and then you die 24 hours later. Why go on?"

The counsellor looked at Enid with great consternation. He was old; in fact, he probably had less than an hour to live, which made him the wisest and most experienced of all flag flies in the country. "Why are you so unhappy when you have your whole life in front of you?"

Enid stuck out her lip. "Because I'm going to die in less than a day. Do you realize that our species is the shortest lived in the entire insect kingdom?"

"Yes," said the counsellor, "this is true, but the shortness of life does not determine its quality, my young, anxious flag fly. Rather, awareness of one's death makes everything all the more meaningful, all the more special, you see. That is why I believe we are the most truly blessed species in the whole world." The counsellor then took out a pipe and began puffing on it. "Let me tell you a story," he said. Everybody leaned toward the counsellor, waiting for his big words to inspire them. Unfortunately, just as the counsellor was about to speak, he died.

The students were sad for a few seconds, but they only had so many seconds to process their grief. Sadness was soon replaced by anger. They were angry that the counsellor had wasted their therapy time by dying.

"I feel very disturbed by what I saw here today," said Tanya, a very skinny flag fly. "He's the third analyst I've gone through this morning."

"Yeah," said a student called Otto. "The one guy got us thinking about guilt complexes, and then died before the 'freeing ourselves' session."

Enid looked at the anxious flag flies around her. Then she looked at the dead flag fly in front of her. "If only I could extend the life of the flag fly just one more day," she thought to herself. And then, it came to her. She would go to school and become a scientist, a famous scientist that could prolong the lifespan of her species.

Enid quickly dashed off and headed for a school. In fact, she was so much in a hurry to get on with her life that she forgot to tell Bernie where she was going. "I'll catch up with Bernie later," thought Enid.

Enid had spent what would seem to a human being several difficult years in school. Elementary and high school took, in real time, one hour each, and university took two. But as Enid progressed through the school system, she realized her dreams of becoming a great scientist would never happen. There were others who were far brighter than her and who seemed far more capable of inventing a potion to extend the lifespan of the flag fly.

"Oh, what's the point," she cried to her tree mate, Jessie. "I'll never be able to come up with a cure for death."

"So stop trying and have some fun."

"Fun?" The word echoed through her as though someone in her past was trying to reach her. "Bernie," she said out loud.

"Bernie?" said Jessie. "Who's he?"

"Oh, just this guy I liked a long, long time ago."

"Whatever," said Jessie as he donned his leather jacket. "Anyway, there's a party in three minutes in that tree knot. Why don't you come along for the ride?"

Enid had never been to a party before, but she was so sad, she went anyway. Climbing into the tree knot three minutes later, Enid's antennae were met with the sounds of loud buzzing and chirping. There were bugs of all shapes and sizes, some with floating tentacles, others that looked like flying horses. One bug had wrapped himself in a leaf and was recklessly rolling around, crashing into everybody.

"Quite the party, eh?" said the bug.

"I guess so," said Enid as she tried to find a place to sit down.

"Try some of this tree sap," said Freddie, a flag fly with droopy feelers. "It's really fermented."

Enid tasted some and felt all warm and funny inside, "I can't quite see straight."

"Yeah, I can't feel my brain. Isn't it great?" Freddie burped loudly.

Enid felt strange, almost as though she were being put to sleep. "What's in this stuff anyway?" she asked, slurring her words.

A bloated fly rolled past her, said "buzz juice" and then exploded on the side of the tree.

"Gross," cried Enid. "Is this what you guys do in this place, get drunk and explode?"

"Pretty much," said Freddie, who was now crashing into twigs. "You got a better way to kill time?"

Enid looked at her watch. Five hours left.

"Hey, beautiful," said a new flag fly that had just flown into the party. "Wanna get married?" In the flag fly world, the courting ritual usually consisted of one or two well-placed pickup lines.

Enid was dumbfounded. She had never thought about the idea of marriage, although she had often heard other flies talk about getting married after they finished school.

"Come on," said the flag fly. "You're not getting any younger."

Enid looked at the clock again. If only she hadn't been so foolish that minute so long ago in the forest. If only she had told Bernie what she needed to say. But now, it was too late. Bernie was gone.

"Come on, get married. You know ya wanna," shouted the other drunk flag flies. Wiping a tear out of her eyes, Enid said the vow of fertility, and the two were married a second later. The two quickly built a nest in the grass. For a time, Enid was happy. She had what other people called the perfect life: a house, a husband and 127 teeny, tiny, perfect little eggs.

Things began to change, however, in her twentieth hour. Enid's husband became lazy and expected her to do all the housework. And because she had worked so hard for so long, she began to look and feel old.

"I'm leaving you for a younger flag fly," her husband announced.

"But why?" asked Enid. "An hour ago, you said I was beautiful."

"An hour ago you were, and I still had five hours left," he replied.

Watching her husband fly away, Enid began to cry. Nothing had worked out the way she expected. Everything she had struggled for was in vain. She began to wonder if she should ever have left that hole in the ground, after all.

"Enid?" said a soft voice behind her. "Enid! It's me." She turned toward the voice.

Enid's sad face immediately began to brighten. "Bernie?"

Like Enid, Bernie had aged considerably. His high, squeaky voice was now low and raspy. His knees were now bent in the wrong direction, and a bird had nipped off one of his feet.

"I looked everywhere for you, Enid," said Bernie.

Tears began to well up in Enid's eyes.

Then Bernie said in a steady voice, "Did you find what you were looking for?"

Enid stretched out her feelers and hugged Bernie. "Yes."

And Enid and Bernie sang and laughed and told stories as they lived out their two remaining hours in a bright, burning splendour . . .

Printed in the United States
131843LV00004B/2/P

9 780595 476916